Runners

a novella

by

Nicholas Cushner

PublishAmerica

Baltimore

© 2004 by Nicholas Cushner.

This book is a work of fiction. Names, characters, places, and incidents are used fictitiously or are products of the author's imagination. Any resemblance to actual persons or locales is purely coincidental.

First printing

ISBN: 1-4137-3935-0
PUBLISHED BY PUBLISHAMERICA, LLLP
www.publishamerica.com
Baltimore

Printed in the United States of America

For Janice

No one can love unless he is impelled by the persuasion of love.

—From: Andreas Capellanus,
De arte honeste amandi, c. 1175

Acknowledgements

I was considerably influenced by several authors who have written eloquently and in a scholarly way about the nature of love and how easily we can fall out of love. Many of their thoughts are scattered throughout *Runners*.
They are:

Helen Fisher, *Why We Love. The Nature and Chemistry of Romantic Love*
John Fiske and Martie Fiske, *Why Do Fools Fall in Love?*
Gabriel García Márquez, *Love in the Time of Cholera*
Shirley P. Glass, *Not "Just Friends"*
William Jankowiak, ed., *Romantic Passion*
Nathaniel Reade, "Love at First Sight," *Attaché (February 2002)*
Susan Shapiro Barash, *A Passion for More*
Gail Sheehy, *Passages. Predictable Crises of Adult Life*
Robert Sternberg, *Love is a Story*
Melanie Thernstrom, "Untying the Knot," *New York Times Magazine*, August 24, 2003

Contents

Part One
La Guardia Airport

one

Billows of steam poured out of the shower and Robyn Taylor, like Sybil coming out of clouds at Delphi, stepped through, drying her hair with the thick turkish towel embossed in blue that had Gramercy Park Hotel on the edge. Alan Powell, propped on a pillow against the headboard, had watched the bathroom door swing open. Robyn stood in front of him just a moment longer than she had to, bending her head, rubbing her wet, dark brown hair and tossing it back gracefully every so often in a movement reminiscent of flirting with someone at a bar. Robyn was an incredibly beautiful woman, the kind that turned heads when she entered a room. She carried herself with an air of confidence. Her clothes, especially tonight, accentuated her figure as well as her cinnamon skin. Robyn's 5'7" frame was athletic, her calves muscular like a runner's, her thighs well developed. Her stomach was almost flat, buttocks tight and hard. She was flat chested and she didn't like jokes about it. Alan once told her that everything over a handful was superfluous. Robyn didn't laugh and Alan never said anything like that again. Her face was oval with dark brown eyes, a soft, light brown complexion with smooth, delicate skin, if she lived in the 1850s she would be classified as mulatta, and she had a long, swan-like neck. Alan felt an overwhelming physical attraction for Robyn, and he wanted to make love to her now more than ever.

When they returned from dinner, she had surprised him by

saying she would take a shower. Robyn shimmied out of her short hunter green sheath dress and slipped into the bathroom. Alan flipped on a rerun of *X-Files*. He unbuttoned his white 15½, 34/35 shirt and hung it in the closet over the blue blazer he wore that evening. He folded his gray trousers over the easy chair and stretched his 6' frame on the bed with only his socks and Jockey shorts on. Alan felt chilly, so he took off his socks, went under the covers and began to watch Agent Mulder.

Alan looked at himself in the full length wall mirror directly opposite the bed: his good-looking face, green eyes and blond tousled hair sticking out of the bed covers made him smile. He looked like a patient in a hospital bed waiting for his dinner.

"Something was lost when they refurbished these old New York hotels," Alan said out loud.

Robyn and Alan dined that evening at *Il Fiorentino* on the corner of 23rd Street and Second Avenue.

The Friday night crowd caused a 45-minute wait for a table so they stayed at the bar until the hostess called them. Alan had a Rob Roy with a twist of lemon. Robyn played with a daiquiri.

"I thought you only drank those at the beach in Mexico," Alan said.

"Anywhere, anytime," she replied.

The table they finally got was next to the ceiling-to-floor glass window facing Second Avenue. The chilly October evening made the single candle on the table seem like a cozy fire. Alan and Robyn's faces glowed in the candlelight as they began to feel the headiness from the drinks. She let him order his favorite wine, *Orvieto Classico*. Alan had an appetizer of *prosciutto* and melon followed by a *risotto milanese*. Robyn ordered fried soft-shell crabs. Just after the coffee appeared, Alan felt Robyn's leg rubbing against his. He pressed his tighter against hers.

They went through Gramercy Park on their way back to the hotel, pausing only long enough to comment on the late-blooming chrysanthemums. At 9 o'clock, when the park guard told them they had to leave, they felt like teenagers being scolded about being out after dark.

Robyn finally let the towel drop and stood in front of Alan for a second, as if saying, "Well, here I am." He lifted the bed covers and when Robyn entered his outstretched arms, he kissed her softly on the lips.

"Mmm, you taste good."

Robyn pulled back. "I think I drank too much tonight," she said. "The daiquiri and then wine."

"No, you didn't."

"How can you say that? I know how much I drank!"

"You drank just enough, and you were ravishing. Every head turned when you walked into the restaurant."

"Silly, nobody even saw me!"

"Are you kidding? How could they not notice that body, those legs?"

Alan leaned back and put out the light behind the bed. The TV kept playing but neither Alan nor Robyn noticed.

two

Next morning Alan and Robyn took a taxi to the Airport Bus Terminal on Park Avenue near Grand Central Station. From the hotel the cabby went straight up Park Avenue.

"The Morgan Library's up there," Alan said, pointing in the direction of Madison Avenue as they crossed 36th Street. Robyn didn't reply but kept staring out the cab window. Was it a silence that came from guilt? Or the "ten-minute syndrome"? Ten minutes after, you regret having done it! Robyn was going to stay in New York for an extra day. Shopping, she said. Alan suspected that she didn't want to return to Boston on the same plane and run the risk of someone seeing them together in Logan Airport, but he didn't say anything. He felt that Robyn wasn't forthright about why she wanted to stay in New York, but it was only a suspicion. He wondered how many more suspicions would cloud his love affair with Robyn Taylor. When Alan began the affair, he thought that he would never sleep with Robyn. He thought he could have an affair without sex, one of those new types of intimacies that had everything without touching her body. He thought that he could be an intimate friend, share so much with her, but never feel her body next to his. But he had formed such a deep connection with Robyn Taylor that he crossed the line from platonic friendship to sexual intimacy. Alan recalled a colleague's remark, that "you lose all credibility with a woman once you've had sex with her." He may have been right. Something had changed, but he wasn't sure what.

The cab pulled up to the curb. Robyn turned to Alan, cupped his head in her hands, and kissed him. He didn't say anything. The cabby had jumped out, opened the trunk, and put Alan's bag on the curb.

"Better get out before it disappears," Robyn said.

Alan nodded, opened the cab door, and stepped into a brilliant blue-sky morning. He went around the rear of the cab, bent down and blew a kiss to Robyn. She smiled and the cab moved forward.

The terminal loudspeaker announced that the bus for LaGuardia was loading.

By the time Alan's bus entered the Queens Midtown Tunnel and emerged in Long Island City, the city's stillness had not yet broken. A few pedestrians were making their way to the newsstand for the Sunday morning paper but the churchgoers had not yet emerged and the light traffic allowed the bus to speed along the Long Island Expressway. But Alan Powell wasn't thinking about traffic or pedestrians. He was recalling every moment of his weekend with Robyn Taylor, from the time he suggested that they meet in New York City.

"It's a Literature Association Meeting. I'd feel out of place," Robyn stammered.

Alan was surprised that she momentarily had lost her composure.

"Oh, you'll be fine. You can go to the Metropolitan or the Village while I go the sessions I have to attend. Then we can meet. And Eric will be in New Orleans, right?"

Alan read the excitement in Robyn's face.

"Eric's first meeting is on Thursday morning, so he'll leave on Wednesday." Robyn's husband was doing an advanced degree in counseling at Tulane University and he was attending one of the required residency weekends in New Orleans.

"It seems so calculating."

"It is. But how do you know what Eric does on his 'study' trips?" Alan rationalized.

So Robyn and Alan took separate planes to New York. His arrived on Thursday at 10:30 a.m. Alan recalled the wad of bills that the collector-driver had in his hand when he boarded the bus that took him from the airport to the city. The trip took about half an hour and Alan got off at Grand Central Station, going directly to the Gramercy Park Hotel, where he had made a reservation for a double room. He arrived too early to occupy the room, the maids hadn't yet cleaned up from the previous night's guests, so he left his bag in the storage room and went uptown to the conference. Thursday night he spent by himself. Robyn arrived at 3 p.m. the next day, going straight to the hotel. Alan met her in the lobby. She wore a dark blue pants suit, the suitcoat cut close to the body, outlining her figure, with an off-white collar shirt, and around her neck was a thin gold chain with a tiny diamond in it. Casual but chic. Robyn never overdressed. Alan remembered his discomfort when they entered room 612. He was going to have to share the bathroom with her, the shower, and the bed. From that time on, whenever he entered a hotel, the room number 612 always popped into his head.

Alan hadn't considered the other side of sharing a room with Robyn. So at around 4:30 a.m. he quietly slid out of the bed in order to shave, brush his teeth, urinate, flush the toilet, and wash. No shower. Then he gently slid back into bed next to the woman whose cadenced breathing kept him awake until the soft light began peeking though the slit between the drapes covering the window. Alan watched Robyn's outline under the sheets. Her face up, breasts heaving slightly, then she abruptly turned away towards the wall, as if to say that she didn't appreciate his watching her.

The airport bus rumbled along and Alan closed his eyes to relive the dark embrace of the previous night. He saw Robyn's brown eyes, heard her gentle voice, and felt her soft skin. Her hands were around his waist and his body, her lips and tongue against his, saying "I love you," as if no other kisses or hands had ever existed. But her quiet words seemed empty, so Alan kissed her hands and her forehead as if to say, "I need you, Don't ever leave me."

"Hey mister. Didn't you want American Airlines?" the bus driver shouted without turning his head. "This is it."

"Right."

Alan had kept his bag with him on the bus and headed for the check-in counter. He was surprised to hear, "This is the final boarding call, American Airlines, Flight 341 to Boston. Please proceed immediately to Gate 7B." He thought that he had left Manhattan with plenty of time to spare. The airline's clerk waved him through. He had only eight minutes before departure.

As Alan entered the plane, he spotted the empty seat 6E on the aisle. He usually felt a certain anticipation over who would occupy the seat next to him. He would watch the passengers one by one enter the plane, guessing, or hoping, who would be his trip companion. On one occasion a young woman sat next to him with long brown hair, wearing a black skirt and a white V-necked sweater over a T-shirt. Probably a graduate student, because she had a copy of the *New York Times* in her left hand. Or a computer-wiz from Wang. Alan imagined running his hand through her hair, sliding it up her sweater sleeve, and watching her fall asleep with her pouting lips invitingly pursed. He wanted to talk to her. However, on this occasion Alan didn't care who sat beside him. He wanted to bury himself in his thoughts. Someone said "Pardon me," and climbed over him.

Alan's quest for silence was successful until the plane was airborne and the flight attendants began serving beverages. A man was seated beside him and he asked the attendant for coffee with no cream. Alan requested a Sprite.

"You live in Boston?"

"Yes, I do."

"Was there a long time ago. Can't remember where Copely Square is. Is it in the center of town?"

"Yes, a few blocks from the Commons."

"I'm going for a sales training meeting, pharmaceuticals. What do you do?"

Alan knew that his answer would reveal the level of his education, his salary range, his social class. His reply would provide the questioner with enough information to calculate his social and economic status. But perhaps the questioner was simply attempting to make small talk.

"I'm a teacher."

"Oh really, what do you teach?"

"Literature."

"Where?"

"Salem State."

"I used to read a lot. Not anymore. Sales reports, *Business Week* and the daily paper now. Are you married?"

"Yes."

"Kids?"

"Two girls."

"That's great. I divorced two years ago. But I see my three kids regularly. Never missed a support payment."

Alan hoped to quiet the man in seat 6E by responding in monosyllables. Only after Alan closed his eyes feigning sleep did he stop asking questions.

three

American Airlines Flight 341 droned upwards over Rockaway Bay. Alan Powell's quasi-sleep gently descended to a state of half-sleep. The memories of the weekend kept entering his semi-conscious, perching, fluttering away, returning, soaring, like the pigeons of St. Mark's. One memory brought Alan all the way back to his first encounter with Robyn Taylor. Alan was a jogger, and so was she.

Alan ran like the marathoner, Alberto Salazar, with soles parallel with the ground, ever since he tripped and spread-eagled his six-foot frame into the hard summer dirt, scraping his knees and the palms of his hands. He always gave a wide berth to the twisted wood sticking out of the ground on the eastern side of the Back Bay Fens Park next to the zoo. He didn't want to have to look up again at the passing joggers shouting at him, "You OK?"

Alan smelled the buffaloes every time he ran along the east side of the park. So did his chocolate lab, Rufus, who at this spot in the morning jog always pointed his head in the zoo's direction while running straight ahead as if expecting the herd to charge out at him through the slits of their iron cage. The zoo entrance gate across the road (the jogging path was along the inside edge of the road) was flanked by a concrete life-sized lion and a polar bear. Twenty yards beyond the entrance twelve bison in an outdoor pen surrounded by a high steel fence were bent over as still as statues with only their jaws moving from

21

side to side. "They should be out running. An hour a day around the park would be great for them. What a sight!" Alan thought.

In August Alan ran at about 6:30 in the morning to escape the heat and before the golfers descended on the nine holes that occupied the center of the park. Alan did not appreciate the golfers turning Frederick Law Olmsted's masterpiece into a golf course.

Even the snows of January and February did not deter him from his daily run. The winter wind created giant drifts on the east side of the park in front of the zoo. But someone always beat down a narrow path, allowing the hardiest of the winter joggers to run past the bison, all of whom from December on had white crusty beards. Alan admired the bison. They had a noble quality.

Rufus never paid serious attention to the bison. By the time Alan and Rufus reached that side of the park, Rufus was tired and less likely to go barking after the buffaloes. Alan let Rufus run loose. It was too early for the police car to make its rounds so he was not afraid of getting a summons for allowing Rufus to run unleashed. Rufus always ran alongside Alan ever since he got lost sniffing around the tennis courts for the green balls that the tennis players looped over the iron fence. The balls always settled under the leaves and Rufus's proudest moment was when he ascended from a pile of flaky brown leaves with a green ball held tightly in his mouth. Rufus's vet once told Alan that she frequently had to extract tennis balls from dogs' stomachs, usually in the summer, so Alan was afraid that Rufus in his excitement would swallow the ball. He never did.

Rufus got lost that day because he became so involved rummaging for tennis balls and Alan was so intent on his running that by the time Rufus looked for Alan, he was gone, and vice versa. Although Rufus was supposedly a smart dog, he did a lot of dumb things. On that day he ran looking for Alan in the opposite direction. Alan grew more and more frantic, asking the few joggers out that early if they saw a chocolate lab running around alone.

Finally one jogger shouted, "I saw one on the other side of the park."

Alan took off diagonally across the grass, past the stone that marked the spot where the hospital was during the Civil War, past the giant oak tree in the geographic center of Olmsted's park, and shouting as loud as he could, "Rufus, Rufus," every ten seconds or so. Racing through Alan's mind as he ran was one thought, How could I tell the kids that I lost the dog? What am I going to say to them? Finally, Alan saw Rufus, standing still on the little hill near the golf house, watching as he ran towards him. Rufus recognized Alan and they ran to each other. Alan was angry, annoyed at himself for not paying more attention to Rufus, but also happy that he found his dog. Rufus wagged his tail and probably wondered what the big deal was. But ever since then, he stuck close to Alan during his run in the park.

The circumference of the jogging trail was 2.3 miles. Alan could do no more than one lap. Before his hernia surgery, he used to do six laps around the park on Saturday afternoons. He was certain that the surgery affected his running.

Meg, his wife, disagreed. "It's in your head," she used to say. "The surgery has nothing to do with running less." He respected what Meg had to say about his health.

Meg never liked running in the park. Nor did she use the Nordic-Trac she had at home. She kept trim by careful eating and an occasional summer evening stroll with Alan around the block, or sometimes around the park. To Alan she was amazing. She could eat the sinfully delicious chocolate cake at the local sweets shop, *Sweet Tooth,* with no apparent weight increase. Her waist was as narrow as the day they were married.

"You must have sold your soul to keep that waist," Alan

used to tell her.

Meg would smile as though there were really some trick to it that she was hiding from him. "Slim•Fast," she would reply.

Alan never found any Slim•Fast in the pantry.

The morning when Alan first met Robyn began like a hundred other mornings in the Back Bay Fens. The park was almost empty. Only the early morning regulars were churning around the running path: Ray Hart, the spindly retired steelworker, Mel Moseby walking with his old friend whom Alan never met. The others were too far away to identify. Rufus made for his favorite spot in the dewy grass after he leaped from the cargo compartment of Alan's green Chevy Blazer. Alan scooped up Rufus's droppings in one of the three plastic bags he kept in the fanny-pack around his waist, put the bag into one of the large trash barrels that were around the running path, and began walking towards the interior of the large green oval. Alan decided to run on the grass even though he knew it was dangerous. He could easily twist an ankle on a root or stone or throw out a muscle in one of many slight depressions within the oval. But the air was crisp, the sun just beginning to peek through the branches of the trees on the eastern edge of the park, and he liked the idea of his feet hitting the soft grass. It was also easier on his knees. Besides, it was too beautiful a morning for anything bad to happen.

The sound of muffled voices came from the entrance by the zoo. Alan turned and saw some people, he could only see the figures, out with their pets. Alan was not surprised. He frequently saw the same group (at least he thought it was the same group) at the zoo entrance to the park this early in the morning. Alan continued towards the interior of the park and then began to jog in a clockwise direction. Rufus was confused. They always ran in the *other* direction. But Rufus realized that this morning he was going in *this* direction, so he took off ahead of Alan sniffing for squirrels or golf balls, then running, sniffing some more, then catching up to Alan.

On the southeast side of the park giant elms overhung the running path, and just beyond the elms was a fully accessible outdoor set of adult athletic equipment. Parallel bars, chin presses, arm rungs for strengthening, each item with detailed instructions for use stretched for about a hundred yards paralleling the running path. Alan never noticed that the set had been erected (suddenly it just appeared with no notice at all), nor had he ever seen anyone using the equipment this early in the morning. A century ago the running path had been a horse path where the elite of the city sauntered sidesaddle or fully mounted for an afternoon ride. Many households had carriage houses and stables where horses were kept. Now the horses were forbidden entrance to the park and the runners had taken over.

"You better put a leash on that dog. The police car is coming around!"

The warning came from the group of walkers that Alan had seen at the zoo entrance. They were now approaching him, three women, and as they did so, each face became more distinct and well-defined. The voice came from the woman in the center of the group, the one in a gray running suit with a thin red stripe around the collar and along the sides of the form-fitting pants. Alan recognized it as an expensive suit, the kind he saw advertised in *Runner's World* for over $150. Her face was attractive, light brown complexion, hair pulled tight around her head by a two-inch wide red headband that wound around her ears and forehead. She was tall, about three inches over any of her partners, and she was in excellent shape, at least from what Alan saw. She carried one of those retractable leashes in her hand that Alan referred to as a "Yuppie" leash. He remembered an *Animal Planet* TV program about dog leashes and the narrator explained that retractable leashes were not appropriate for 70-90-lb. dogs. A leather leash with a loop at the end afforded more control. But the retractable leashes were the "in" thing.

"What about him?" Alan shouted back. "You should have that killer Golden on a leash!"

Alan pointed at the dog walking alone on the other side of the running path. He presumed that she was the owner.

"Casco's harmless."

"Tell that to the cop."

She laughed.

The woman's walking partners didn't say anything during the exchange. They held on to their own dogs a bit more tightly but they smiled at the banter and saying something to each other that Alan could not understand.

In an instant the encounter was over.

The path was slightly downhill on this side of the park. Rufus was off to his right, still sniffing for the unobtainable squirrel. When Alan got to a level spot he stopped and tied his right shoelace that was coming undone. He glanced back to see the three figures turning the curve at the top of the incline.

Alan continued his jog but when he reached the area near the Blazer where he would normally stop, he kept jogging.

Think I'll go around again, he thought. Rufus wagged his tail.

Alan thought about a clever remark to make to the nameless woman walker with the Golden Retriever. He rehearsed a couple but they didn't satisfy him. Instead, he passed the zoo entrance without meeting the walkers again. They got there before he did and had exited the park.

Next morning Alan woke up thinking about his run in the park. Not the run but whether he would see the woman he had spoken to in the park the morning before.

"Hey, you getting up?" Meg asked, leaning over to his side of the bed. "No coffee delivery today?"

Alan turned and kissed her on the forehead. "I always

wanted to be a houseboy," he said.

He caught himself wondering whether he would ever again see the woman with the Golden Retriever. While discussing *The Divine Comedy* in his literature class, the nameless face from the park kept replacing Beatrice. Alan thought of Jay Leno's bobbing face playing Ditondo on *The Late Night Show*. After classes, he returned home, started boiling the water for broccoli and checked the pot roast he had put in the oven that morning on Timed Bake. As always, the family ate dinner together with candles on the table.

Kristin talked about Mr. Rodgers, her physics teacher.

"Too bad you don't have a woman physics teacher," Meg said.

"That wouldn't make any difference. I'd still hate the smells in the lab."

"I thought that the smells were in the chem lab."

"We use the same one."

Vicky was not up to the banter of her sister. The difference in ages had widened to a yawning chasm now that Kristin was a high school junior and Vicky a lowly freshman.

"And you, kiddo," Alan said to Vicky, "what did Mrs. Flynn have to say in social studies today?"

"Not much. Bobby Driscoll got into trouble because of the note he sent Dierdre."

And then Vicky launched into a blow-by-blow description of Bobby's interest in his co-freshman at JFK High School.

After she finished, Meg said firmly, "I really believe that boys and girls should be in different classes, if not in different schools! I really believe they should."

"Why?" Vicky and Kristin asked almost in unison, and with a hurt expression as if it were going to happen the next day.

"Because you kids pay more attention to what the Bobby Driscolls of the class think than to your studies."

Alan stayed out of the discussion. He knew that Meg firmly

27

believed that same-sex classes would improve female science and math scores. Something, he used to say, she had learned in the sixties. He had often countered that schools should reflect the world that the girls would live in, so prepare for it. Meg would have none of it. If she could afford it, she would have both Kristin and Vicky enrolled at Boston Academy, a girls-only school. But she couldn't, so JFK, with its massive, personality-less, yellow-brick façade, its institutional-like corridors and locker rooms, and its cavernous cafeteria, was where the girls attended school.

"Oh Mom," was all that Vicky could say.

After dinner the girls ran upstairs to finish homework and watch the hour of television they were permitted on Tuesday evenings.

Alan had cooked so Meg washed. He cleared the table and put away the dishes. When he finished he stayed downstairs, paging through the first section of the *Boston Globe,* halfheartedly reading about Ronald Reagan's latest effort at trickle-down economics and Gorbachev's rejoinder to the U.S. president's "Evil Empire" remark. But Alan's thoughts were continually being pulled to the following morning as he played out different scenarios in a possible encounter with the Golden Retriever lady. What if she didn't even look at him? Or pay any attention? Should he stop and chat? Suppose she knows somebody that I know? What if she doesn't show up?

"Alan," Meg interrupted from upstairs.

"What?" he answered.

"Don't forget to send the car insurance check tomorrow. It's overdue."

"Don't worry, I will."

It was close to one o'clock when Alan went upstairs and slipped under the covers. Meg was already sleeping.

The autumn of 1986 was capriciously cold in New England—from New Hampshire, where the edges of Lake

Keansaw almost froze, to the Connecticut River Valley, where the hibiscus stiffened in the early frost. Local orchards and gardens lost their fruit and flowers and when early snow fell in November, it stayed longer on the ground because the earth and the concrete were already cold.

When Alan rose next morning, the windows were coated with frost, so he went over to see if there was snow on the ground. There was none. The thermostat stayed at 55 during the night so the house felt frigid when everybody got up in the morning. The night before, he set the automatic Mr. Coffee to start perking at 6 a.m. Alan was usually the first one up, calling Kristin and Vicky while making his way to the kitchen.

Alan roused the girls, poured the ritual mugs of coffee, brought one to Meg, and began to put on his running togs: a tight fleece-lined sweatshirt under a bulkier sweatshirt with the green and yellow symbol of the International Club of Salem State, a pair of Gore-Tex running pants, and a dark blue canvas fanny-pack for Rufus's plastic bags and for Alan's keys. He pulled on his Sauconys. It was chilly enough for gloves and a hat so Alan put on a pair of thin orange work gloves and the navy blue watch cap that Meg called "a mugger's cap." By then the girls were making toast in the kitchen and Meg was in the shower.

"I'm going," Alan shouted up the stairs to Meg. "See you tonight."

The girls said so long and Alan was off.

Back Bay Fens Park was bathed in white light when Alan arrived. The park was silent. The sun was just coming up behind the bare elm trees on the park's eastern rim. Alan and Rufus started out clockwise on their morning jog. Nobody was visible but all of a sudden a lone runner began approaching down the long path next to the zoo, a white ball of rising sun behind his back, his breath condensing in the cold morning air like Rufus's. If the runner had had long whiskers, they would be frozen. Alan halted for a second to take in the sight of the lone approaching runner. Rufus paid no attention. The runner passed.

Alan spotted three distant figures rounding the curve on the eastern edge of the park. A flash of grey and red told him that one of them might be her. Alan's jog turned into a walk. Rufus was off to the right. When the figures were about fifty yards away, he was positive that it was her. Alan bent down, untied his right shoelace and took his time retying it. They were close enough to talk.

"Hey, the animal walkers," he shouted. "Where's your dog?" Alan directed his question to the woman he had been thinking about the day before.

"Over there. Sniffing away." She pointed to the grass across the path. The Golden Retriever was on the other side of the road.

The three women slowed down.

Alan glanced at the woman's walking partners, realizing in a split second that he should bring them into the conversation too.

He spoke to the woman with the black poodle. "What's his name?"

"Millie. It's a her."

Alan smiled. The third woman was petless. She seemed bashful, just smiling as the other two began talking.

Alan's attention returned to the woman with the Golden Retriever. Dogs have a way of becoming the centerpiece of a conversation, a neutral diversion, a third party to focus attention on.

"Casco's face is so white. Like a little old man," Alan said. He remembered the dog's name.

"He's getting up there."

"How old is he?"

"Nine. He'll be ten in January."

Alan was embarrassed. He was actually speaking with her. He felt ill-at ease because of the presence of the other two so he cut short the conversation.

He began to move away but the friendly smile of the Golden Retriever lady kept him riveted on her.

"Take care. See ya later."

They waved.

Alan renewed his jog. The sun was bright and warm but the air was cool. He didn't even know her name. Thinking of her as the Golden Retriever lady made it all the more mysterious. But what was the "it"? A mild flirtation? Ridiculous. He was married with a wonderful wife and two great kids. Alan returned home, trying to leave the idea behind in the park. But it stayed with him all that day with the same gray color, the same tremulous wings, fluttering around, refusing to leave.

four

Robyn Taylor left the park in her black Honda civic. She lived in a little red brick house on Essex Street with her husband and six-year-old daughter, Emily. Robyn traveled the same route every day, up Boyleston, along Park Drive, and past Beacon Street. But this time was different. She was in a hurry because she told Eric that she would take their daughter to her recital practice.

As Robyn pulled into the driveway, Eric was getting into his little red convertible BMW. Emily was standing at the doorway. He blew a kiss towards Robyn and took off.

"Mom, I have to be at practice in a half hour."

"Don't worry, hon, you'll be there on time."

"Miss Peters really gets annoyed if we're late."

"I know. Don't worry. We'll go in a couple of minutes. Did you have any cereal, or fruit?"

"Yes."

Emily was practicing for a class singing recital, and even though it was a holiday, there was a teachers meeting, a practice was scheduled.

Emily followed her mother into the house and as they went towards the upstairs bathroom so that Robyn could take a quick wash, Emily said, "Dad told me that you would take me this morning."

"I know. Give me one minute, and we're off."

Emily was diagnosed with dyslexia. At least that's what the

principal at the Newton School said. So Eric and Robyn searched out a learning environment that was more relaxed and informal. They found one, had the financial resources to enroll her, and decided to keep her there until they learned whether she really was dyslexic. They still had doubts.

Robyn got back into the car with Emily beside her. They latched their seatbelts and off they went.

"What time will I pick you up?"

"We'll be finished around noon."

The drive to Emily's school was a short one, but as she drove Robyn thought about the owner of Rufus. She thought about how obvious his chance encounter was. The chance encounter was no chance encounter at all. It was deliberate. She'd have to call her friend Rhonda about him some time this morning. Rhonda had more insight into men's motivations than she had.

She pulled up next to the school. Emily kissed her quickly and bolted out of the car.

"See you at noon," Robyn shouted.

At the first red light Robyn flipped down the vanity mirror. No gray strands that needed a Clairol touch-up. Still pretty at 43! Still the mysterious mulatta! And why not? Her morning run, along with a bit, just a bit, of dieting, kept her slim and attractive to males. Even if Eric didn't notice her the way she wanted him to. She flipped the mirror back into place.

Robyn chose to stay with Eric even though she knew his eyes and body wandered elsewhere. Stability (home, family, house), was that what it was, over freedom. But freedom for what?

Her first marital escapade was with Richard, Sir Richard the Dentist, she called him. She began the affair out of spite, to get even with Eric for *his* affair with the nurse. Richard was wealthy. He drove a Mercedes LX and had a spacious apartment in a high-rise on the eleventh floor overlooking the harbor. At first she made wild love with Richard in his kingsize sleigh bed. But over time, Robyn realized that one's bed was for love, not love affairs, so she began to fake the tender embraces as well as the gasping and moaning that accompanied the sexual gymnastics. Robyn used to call Richard at his office in Newton every Tuesday at two. The calls diminished. Every two weeks, every four weeks, and eventually they separated.

Robyn's second affair was with George. He moved too fast. George wanted to set Robyn up in a high-rise on Delaware Avenue next to the Episcopal Church Home. He also gave Robyn a large, rose-scented candle that he claimed he bought from the Cape Cod Candle Shop in Brewster, but she saw them for sale in Pier One. Her affair with George was over before it began.

Robyn wasn't on the prowl. Nor was she looking for someone to replace Eric. She was curious about the runner in the park, the man whose name she didn't know. She was curious about just what was going on in his head. At least, that's what she told herself.

Part Two
Montauk Point

five

Alan opened his eyes when he heard the crackling of the loudspeaker followed by the monotone pilot's voice.

"Folks, we're just going over Montauk Point. You can see the beach from the left-hand side of the plane. Looks like we have clear weather all the way to Boston. Temperature in Boston is 58 degrees. So sit back, relax, and enjoy the flight."

The man in Seat 6E had finished his coffee and was looking at the in-flight AA magazine. He sensed that Alan was awake.

"I can't sleep on planes. Not even in moving cars. Must be something in my sense of balance."

Alan didn't respond.

"How was New York?"

"I spent most of my time at a literature conference. We meet every year."

The man in Seat 6E had no right to be privy to all of his activities.

"Sounds like *our* meetings. The best thing about them is the networking. Never know how somebody is going to help you out down the line."

Alan knew that that was also true for his literature meetings. Sounding out new job opportunities, renewing friendships, and cultivating new buddies at the bar was more important than listening to wannabe scholars drone on about their esoteric research.

"No fun time?"

As much as Alan didn't want to engage in conversation, he sensed a genuineness in the man in 6E. The salesman had removed his dark blue suit coat and put it in the overhead bin. He was about 6', with strong blue eyes, a generous mouth, and a thin, curved nose.

"Not all work," was all that Alan could manage. He said nothing about the surge of excitement he felt returning to the Gramercy Park Hotel to meet Robyn Taylor and of course nothing about the dinner at *Il Fiorentino's*, or walking through the park, or making love to Robyn.

"How long you been married?"

Alan had to think for a second. "Fourteen years."

"Wife from Boston?"

"We met there when we were in graduate school."

"Tell me, did you ever think, why her? Out of all the women you met, why was she the one you chose?"

Alan was startled at the sophisticated nature of the question. He hadn't expected to hear it from the pharmaceutical salesman in Seat 6E.

"Maybe she chose me, not the other way around. Or we chose each other." Whatever equation Alan used, the puzzle remained. "That's a tough question to answer," Alan admitted.

The man in Seat 6E pushed the button that made his seat recline. But he didn't close his eyes. He kept nodding his head in agreement. "It is. So maybe you were attracted to her because she was short and you were tall. Or because you didn't like sports and she was sort of boyish with short hair."

"You sound like a psychologist, or a counselor!"

"Neither. I saw a lot of shrinks in my day. Especially when I was going through my divorce."

Alan noted how he said "my" divorce, as though everyone had one, like a pet poodle.

"I don't know what attracted me to my wife. Her name is

Meg, by the way. There were a lot of other women out there who were more attractive sexually, but we seemed to hit it off."

Alan began to realize that he never really had thought about why he had been attracted to Meg. He just knew that he had been and she was the one he wanted to make his wife. And vice versa.

Meg was the only daughter in a modest-of-means anglophile family from Orange County, New York. Her world opened up when she met Alan in Boston. The theater, baking bread, music, literature, and even the fine points of wine were new to her.

A major attraction for Alan was Meg's ability to function as an independent woman. Except when her mother was around. Then Meg reverted to a more dependent role, even allowing her mother to make decisions that she would never have allowed Alan to make. At first Alan thought that Meg was being practical, preferring not to create problems with her mother. Then he realized that her mother's presence actually altered the way she behaved. He noticed this for the first time when they told her parents that they were going to get married. They had come to visit for Thanksgiving, driving all the way from Greenwood, North Carolina, where they had a retirement condo facing a golf course. Meg's mother was delighted that someone was finally "going to take care of my daughter," and, after two glasses of white *Concha y Toro,* said as much to Alan.

Alan's reply, "I always thought that Meg could take care of herself," was not appreciated.

"Oh, you know what I mean."

Alan really didn't know what she meant. But he could make a good guess.

Meg's dad didn't say very much during Thanksgiving dinner. He commented on how pleasant the table looked, how well cooked the turkey was, and how much Meg had learned from her mother about getting around the kitchen. At first he

39

was a little suspicious of Alan. His world had been within the corporate limits of the IBM complex near Poughkeepsie, New York, where the corporate culture required shirts and ties and even socks that were attached to garters so they appeared straight when you lifted your trousers a bit. Those were the days before the computer nerds took over the corporate computer culture. Meg's father had been "downsized" soon after IBM lost the war to Microsoft. He did receive a little gold watch with "In gratitude for 28 years of exemplary service to IBM" engraved on the back. And he also got a golden parachute to ease his descent to earth. That enabled him to sell the house and buy the golf condo in Greenwood. Meg's mother went along with him. She never had a career outside of the house. Raising Meg was job enough but sometimes she felt like the boutonniere in her husband's lapel. When they got married in 1946, women didn't have careers outside the home. They had replaced the men in factories during World War II but after the war they had to return home. So Meg's father felt that if Meg wasn't married by 31, she would never get married. He too was happy that someone was going to marry Meg, but a teacher in a small college was not the kind of son-in-law he had hoped for. But given her age he was content that at least she was getting married.

Meg's father ticked off Alan at dinner by saying "If you can't do, you teach." He was just trying to be humorous, but Alan didn't like it when the humor was at his expense. Alan felt like reminding him that a "downsized" retiree is not the best judge of successful careers but he just smiled and kept quiet.

Meg was living in an apartment in Brookline the Thanksgiving that Meg's parents visited. It was too small to put both of them up so they stayed in the Radisson near Faneuil Hall.

After Thanksgiving dinner, when her parents left, both Alan and Meg cleaned up the dishes and the kitchen. Meg was happy with the way things went. Her mother and father seemed to get along reasonably well with Alan and they seemed happy at the prospect of having a wedding to look forward to. She was relieved that there were no flare-ups. Alan stayed over that night but they were so tired and stressed out that they only got halfway through their lovemaking.

In early April, Alan and Meg got married in a little chapel in Brattleboro, Vermont. They had come across it on one of their skiing trips and thought it would be a great place to tie the knot. Also its out-of-the way location might reduce the number of guests. It didn't. So Meg in a flowing white dress and Alan in a tuxedo that was a tad too small promised each other to love, obey, cherish, and revere from that day forward.

Three weeks after the wedding, Meg's father had a biopsy taken for his prostate and a week later he learned that he had prostate cancer. Alan tried to interpret Meg's dad's behavior over Thanksgiving and the wedding in the light of his illness. The symptoms of the cancer must have been bothering him while he was in Boston. Meg once told Alan that her father's greatest coping mechanism was denial. He had suffered a minor stroke when he was 49 years old but he never admitted to having had a stroke. It was a "virus." The denials caught up with him. Two years after the diagnosis he died.

Meg and Alan went to the funeral, a non-denominational service arranged by the funeral home near Greenwood.

After her dad died, Meg grew closer to her mother. Meg called her two or three times a week and during one particularly emotional phone conversation invited her to come to Boston to live.

"I spoke with my mother last night."

"Oh, how's she doing?"

"Not too good, I think."

"Anything in particular?"

"Not really. She's just finding it so difficult to live alone.

41

She reaches over in bed and Dad's not there anymore. She hasn't even cleaned out the closets yet. His clothes are still where they were the day he died."

"Don't push her too hard. Let her find her own way through this."

"I'm not pushing her. But some of her behavior seems unhealthy."

"You can't say anything's unhealthy until long after. Give her time."

"I told her she could come to Boston if she wanted to."

"What did she say?"

"Nothing. But she did say that she didn't want to inflict herself on us."

"That sounds like she might take you up on the offer. I'm surprised you didn't say anything to me before asking her that."

Alan really thought that it would be a bizarre thing to do. They were just beginning their own lives together and Alan didn't like the idea of her mother hovering over them.

"I think we have to talk about your mother."

"What about my mother?"

"Well, if she comes to live with us, I think we'll have to set time limits."

"I know that."

"I mean the length of time she should stay here."

"I know what you mean."

"I'm not saying she shouldn't come. Just that if she does, it's not for good."

"I don't know if she'll ever come. I really don't want her to. But she's in pain."

"Maybe the best thing for all of us is to help her adjust to her new situation. Create the things around her that will help her get through this. She's going to have to get used to being alone."

Meg didn't answer. She realized the implications of her

mother's moving in with them and she didn't like them any more than Alan did. But as the only child, she felt she had to reach out to her.

Meg's tenderness was also a quality that attracted Alan. He felt her sensitivity even when they first met in the fall of 1975 at Prof. Lougran's party. His colleague, Joe Fisher, had a crush on Meg and he asked him to invite her over. Alan was there because he recently had jumped the final hurdle in the Ph.D. program and was networking/job hunting. Meg was writing a dissertation on how children learn. He was looking for a teaching position in Comparative Literature in the Boston area, but not many openings existed for a literature man interested in Dante and medieval Italian. Alan was wearing the flared pants that John Travolta had made almost *de rigueur*. His facial hair, Meg later reminded him, made him look like wolfman. Meg wore a straight up-and-down shift that didn't accentuate her curves, thereby forcing the male to pay attention to her brains, not her body. But Meg had it both ways at the party. She deliberately stood in front of one of the living-room lamps so that the males would notice her curves through the dress. Alan later accused her of provoking him. "It wasn't you I was after, lover boy," she told Alan years after. Meg never revealed who she was after.

"So what are you working on?"

"Psychology."

"Oh. A knee-knocker. How many rats eat the cheese."

"That's not how I thought of myself. Experimental Psych is different from the kind of thing I'm doing."

"And what's that?"

"How children learn."

"That's obvious, isn't it? Kids learn by observation and imitation."

"No. They don't."

"Tell me what I missed in Psych 101."

43

"Learning's an active process, not a passive one."

"They have to have something to start with, don't they?"

"They already have."

The tone of Alan's voice told Meg that he wasn't asking questions to impress her or show her up.

"It's like this," she continued, "take a little child who wants a drink of water. The child asks mom for water but mom is busy. So the child goes into the kitchen. She's not tall enough to reach the faucet. You know that my plumber's name is Faucet? Weird! Anyway, the child then climbs onto the sink. Can't reach it. Pulls over the chair. Climbs up and then realizes that she has no glass. Goes to the cabinet where the glasses are kept. Can't reach the shelf where the glasses are. She pulls over a stool. It's tall enough. She gets the glass, pulls the stool back to the faucet, turns on the water, drinks and her thirst is gone. The child has associated new information with satisfying a need. And it worked. No imitation! You cut class the day your prof explained that."

"I had a Teaching Assistant for Psych 101."

"That explains it."

Three months after Meg got her degree in Educational Psychology, on April 7, 1975, she married Alan. Soon after, the Brookline School District hired her as a Curriculum Consultant while Alan was still trying to land a job teaching literature. He finally found a replacement position at Salem State College. Although Meg and Alan agreed that they should find a new place to live after they were married and not move into either of their old apartments, economics forced them to move into Meg's place in Brookline. They turned one of the bedrooms into a shared workplace; three-foot-high green ferns divided the room. Meg gave some of her furniture to the Salvation Army. Alan moved most of his in and Daniel, Meg's nine-year-old Collie-German Shepherd mix, was delighted because he didn't have to move.

44

In June Daniel got sick, just as they were ready to leave for a week in Truro near Provincetown on the Cape. Alan woke up during the night, stretched over towards Meg's side of the bed and woke with a start because she wasn't there. He went downstairs and found her sitting against the wall watching Daniel twitch, his head and left leg jerking every 20 seconds or so. Meg would lean over and stroke Daniel's head and neck every so often. Daniel relaxed when she did that. Alan left her with Daniel and went back to bed without saying anything. Next day Alan and Meg had to carry Daniel into the car and bring him to the vet. The vet couldn't figure out why Daniel was ill. Maybe a stroke. Daniel's condition worsened and the next day Meg insisted on bringing Daniel back to the apartment. She put him on the big plaid-covered dog bed she bought at L.L. Bean's.

When Alan and Meg were at the kitchen table that evening deciding whether to leave the next day for Truro, Daniel dragged himself into the room. His two rear legs didn't function. He plopped down next to Meg. She stroked his head and within a few minutes, Daniel closed his eyes and died.

Meg herself called the Pine Hill Pet Cemetery and made arrangements to bury Daniel. Meg placed Daniel in a burlap sack, carried Daniel down to the car with Alan's help, but insisted that she go alone to the cemetery. She was not crying, but her eyes were teary. She returned an hour later and began to sob uncontrollably.

When Meg had Kristin, Alan jokingly told her that the baby was replacing the Daniel in her life. Meg didn't think the remark was funny.

The birth of Kristin caused the first major rift in Meg and Alan's marriage. Alan never realized how much his remarks about Kristin at birth hurt Meg. Kristin wasn't a beautiful baby when she emerged from Meg. Alan didn't know that no baby at birth was.

"She has a cone head. It's pointed. Do all babies have cone heads?"

"Molding is the proper term. If you had to travel down a birth canal, and you did, you might have the same head shape. She'll grow out of it."

"Look at her squashed little face. Is that normal?"

Meg dismissed the remarks as those of a first-time father. But she never forgot them.

Much more serious was Alan's surprise that a resumption of their sex lives soon after Kristin's birth was impossible. When he whispered sweet nothings into Meg's ear, the reply was, "Do you hear the baby crying?" Dinner and dancing were replaced by dinner and the dishes. His tender caresses were answered with a reassuring pat on the back, and passionate kisses turned into muffled yawns.

"How can you expect me to be a hot mama after spending all day being Mommy?"

"I'm not expecting anything. You're still married to me, aren't you?"

"I'm really tired at night. Can't you understand that?"

"It's already been six weeks since you had Kristin. Isn't that time enough?"

"No, it isn't. It hurts when you put your 180 lbs. on top of my vagina and breasts. I'm stretched, bruised, and tender. Still."

"Maybe we ought to see a sex therapist or a counselor?"

"Hey. We have a baby to share. Love isn't sex, is it?"

"No, it isn't. But you give all your time to the baby. I feel like the odd man out."

"I don't give all my time to the baby. You're my husband and I love you."

"And I love you, too."

"So. What do we do?"

Each took the other's remarks to heart. She understood that

they were now a threesome so she and Alan had to search out opportunities to be alone together; a quiet dinner when the baby was sleeping; the old candle, wine, and soft music routine actually worked. Twice a week Meg brought Alan coffee in bed. She even left a love note in the corduroy jacket he always wore on Tuesdays. On his part, Alan pushed the carriage proudly around the block. He changed Kristin as though he had done it for a living. Meg was delighted to see Alan smitten with his daughter. Eventually Meg ordered some new lingerie from Victoria's Secret.

Meg invited Alan home for "lunch". It was a Thursday and Alan had a meeting with a student at 2:30 p.m. He suspected something. Alan entered the apartment, the bedroom door was ajar, and he saw Meg with a "come-hither" look sitting on the edge of the bed dressed in a floorlength lace nightgown open down the front. Two glasses of wine were on the nightstand.

"Mommy and Daddy, what are you doing?" the baby would have said if she could talk.

Victoria was born a year after Kristin. Her arrival and early years were far less upsetting.

December 6, 1981

Dear Kristin,

I welcome this opportunity to express my love for you on your sixth birthday.

As I write this letter, my thoughts go back to the time you were a tiny, tiny little girl. You have filled my life with so many happy memories. I remember when your mother held you so tightly

---

when we returned from the Brookline Hospital. It was snowing so she wrapped you in a blanket so that only your little head stuck out. I'll never forget the first steps you took in the living room grabbing the back of the rocker after the first two small steps. You grew into such a happy child. The years flew by so fast and soon you were getting ready to go to school. I'll never forget the first day that your mother and I took you to kindergarten. It was the beginning of your journey away from us and toward us. We cried when we got back home.

My hope is that we have given you the wind that will carry you through life, but always by your own path. I hope that you do the things that are really important to you. That you experience all that life's adventures have to offer.

I hope that you keep this letter and, someday when you are older, will read it again. I am proud that you are my daughter and I love you very much.

DAD

six

June 4, 1982

Dear Vicky:

    The years have gone by so quickly that I'm out of breath. One minute you're in diapers and the next you are so grown up!

    I am writing this note on your sixth birthday to tell you how much I love you and how happy I am that you are my daughter.

    Your mother and I are proud of you and our constant wish is that throughout your life you will remain as happy as you are now.

    My hope is that we have given you the wind that will carry you through life, and that you experience all that life's adventures have to offer.

    I hope you keep this letter and when you are older you will read it again.

    With all my love,

DAD

seven

"Why Meg?" Alan sifted through the reasons.

She was attractive, sexually alive, intelligent, enthusiastic, and sensitive. He certainly didn't marry her for her money. She didn't have any. Marrying Meg didn't give Alan "power", nor "status". Then why did he marry her? Love. He married her out of love. He loved her for her kindness. She used to deliver "Meals on Wheels" lunches to the old folk who couldn't fend for themselves. She even showed interest, at least she seemed interested, in Alan's hobby of bird watching. One weekend they went to Gloucester because Meg wanted to see the yellow-bellied sapsucker that was sighted on the rocky coastline. Even after they were married, Meg's sensitivity stuck out, like she was saying, "I love you," every time she did something for Alan. It got to the point where Alan accused her of always wanting affirmation, of always wanting someone to say thank you, of always wanting to please someone. The Cinderella syndrome, he called it. Meg never accepted the analogy.

Meg had offered no objection to his leaving for Europe on study trips even though they separated him from her and the children for lengthy periods and made him feel so guilty that he arranged meeting her in Italy. But guilt was only part of the driving force. She was also a wonderful travel companion. Alan recalled the first time they met in Rome.

Meg, Kristin, and Meg's mother had seen him off at the airport. When Alan opened the carry-on he took with him, he found two large Hershey Bars with nuts and a pack of hard candies with a note from Meg. "Have a Beautiful trip," it said. "See you in ONE week." Alan also felt something hard in the bag. He pulled out a package, opened it and found a copy of H.V. Morton's *Fountains of Rome*. Alan remembered having told Meg once that the *Fountains of Rome* was the only H.V. Morton travel book he had never read. She never let on that she was buying it for him. Meg loved surprises. He wondered how she had gotten hold of the copy. It was long out of print, so maybe she contacted one of those searchers of rare books who advertised in the *New York Times Book Review Section*.

Alan was excited about introducing Meg to Italy, traveling by train to Venice and Florence, and sharing her with no one else. She would be all his. He had pushed the children's strollers so often, changed their diapers, arranged for birthday parties with their friends, watched them when they had colds, cuddled them when they were frightened, that fourteen days in Italy was not too much to ask.

After dinner was served on Alitalia Flight 1289, nonstop Boston to Fiumacino, he dozed off listening to low murmur of the other passengers.

When dawn broke and the plane began to descend, flat, green fields were visible on the right-hand side of the plane. Ostia, the ancient seaport of Rome, was somewhere over there on the right. The plane landed at Leonardo da Vinci Airport but to the Roman it was still Fiumacino, just like to the old-time New Yorker JFK was still Idlewild. Two flight attendants stood by the exit saying to each departing passenger, "Welcome to Rome."

The immigration officer stamped Alan's passport and pointed to the baggage pickup. He collected the gray Samsonite that he always took with him on trips, the one that fell from the luggage rack of his old Chevy station wagon on the Mass Turnpike near Newton. It bounced off the road into the grass.

He was lucky it hadn't hit another car. The only visible sign of the accident was a dent on the top corner near the lock, and it served as an identification mark. Alan passed through customs, boarded the airport bus to the Termini Centrale, where he took the 64 city bus—the pickpocket's special, the Romans called it—to St. Peter's Square. Alan went to the back row and tucked his Samsonite and leather carry-on between his legs.

It was the middle of the morning rush hour, the Rome that Alan loved, alive, bustling, hot, dirty, and beautiful. He was still in that dreamy post-traveling-all-night state as he thought of Graham Geeen's comment about Italians. It was in *The Third Man*. Harry Lime began berating Italy and especially Naples. "They throw offal out the windows. The streets are filled with garbage. Men urinate on the sidewalk. They spit all over. And what has this culture of filth produced? Dante Alighieri, Michelangelo, Rafael, Leonardo da Vinci. And the Swiss, with their antiseptic cleanliness, what was their contribution to world culture? The cuckoo clock!"

Alan repeated variations of the story whenever someone said that Rome was a dirty city or that the Tiber was filthy, or that the canals of Venice were filled with rats.

The bus swung into the Via Nazionale careening down the hill past the Hotel Inglahterra towards the Vittorio Emanuele Monument through traffic that only a New York City cab driver could appreciate. The June sun was already hot at 8:30 a.m. and men were dressed in suits and ties looking like they stepped out of the pages of the *New York Times Sunday Magazine Section*. As the 64 turned right at the Monument, through the Piazza Venezia, Alan caught a glimpse of Trajan's Pillar at the northern end of the Forum. Spewing black fumes from its exhaust, the 64 continued down the Corso Vittorio Emanuele crossing the Tiber over the ornate Puente Emanuele. On his left up the long Via dei Conciliazione that Mussolini built to accommodate his parades, Alan saw the sun reflecting off

Michelangelo's dome, as the bus lurched onto a street parallel to the Via Conciliazione finally stopping alongside the old walls that joined the Vatican to Castel San Angelo, across the street from the Vatican Office for its Secretary of State. Alan waited for everyone to get off. He was in no hurry. From here he would walk to the convent where he was staying.

The daily routine of library, lunch, more study and dinner at around eight o'clock made the week pass quickly. Every day Alan thought of Meg's arrival on Saturday morning. He planned what they would do each of the three days they would be together in Rome, the places they would visit, the restaurants they would go to, even a Pavarotti concert in St. Cecilia's Hall on Sunday afternoon. Tickets cost $70 dollars US, but it was an opportunity he couldn't pass up. Alan went to the American Express office near the Spanish Steps and purchased train tickets and hotel accommodations for Venice and Florence. He and Meg would spend three days in Rome, take the six-hour train ride to Venice, stay there for two nights, then visit Florence, and take the train back to Rome. Finally Friday came. Alan's research work was completed.

Alan set his alarm clock for 4:30 a.m. the morning that Meg was scheduled to arrive. He had spoken to her two days before using the long-distance telephone service in the post office at the foot of the hill where you turn right for St. Peter's Square. The connection was clear. This was her first trip to Europe. She had seven vacation days from school. Her mother would take care of Kristin and she bought $700 in American Express traveler's cheques from the AAA. Her one piece of softside Samsonite luggage, laid out on the bedroom floor all week, was almost packed! Meg told Alan that she went to Brickstone's in the mall and bought a travel coffeemaker that they could use in the mornings when they woke up and she bought packets of Maxwell House coffee and creamer from the local 7-Eleven. Alan kept checking the clock every hour after midnight, so when the alarm sounded, he was wide awake.

His footsteps echoed in the empty street as he made his way down the Viale Vaticano, past the empty entrance to the Sistine Chapel, walking alongside the massive walls that Michelangelo planned for Pope Paul II in 1509. Dawn was just breaking in the east and the stars were still scattered against the dark sky. At the bus stop Alan was grateful that the number 64 bus was there with a solitary driver waiting for the dispatcher's signal to depart at 5:10 for the Termini Centrale. Alan climbed aboard the airport bus to Fiumacino, punched his ticket in the machine that stamped the time of day on it, and sat down in the back. The driver acknowledged his presence. It was too early for conversation. Trucks with vegetables and produce were making deliveries to restaurants, and the motorcycles and cabs were coming to life.

Alitalia Flight 1212, Meg's plane, was on time and scheduled to arrive at 6:45. Alan had 30 minutes. The smell of freshly-brewed coffee drew him to the cafe in the corner of the terminal, and as he sipped his latte Alan watched the growing crowd mulling around the exit of the customs room.

Finally the arrival sign announced that Flight 1212 had landed. The herd-like movement of the crowd reflected the growing excitement and after another twenty minutes the doors of the customs room swung open. Tired-looking travelers began to emerge two and three at a time greeted by shouts followed by the embraces of relatives and friends. With every swing of the door Alan's heart jumped. After what seemed like forty or fifty passengers, Alan became anxious. Where was Meg? Did she miss the plane? Get on the wrong flight? Finally, there she was. Leather shoulder bag swung over her blue Peruvian sweater, weary from the overnight without real sleep, looking over the faces of the greeters, and then she saw him. Alan himself was so excited that he couldn't say anything. He rushed through the crowd and kissed her.

"You're here."

"I can't believe it."

"How was the flight?"

"Good, except the guy next to me talked all night."

"How's Kristin, and Vicky, and your mother?"

"Fine. They took me to the airport. Kristin cried. Mom was great."

Alan stopped in the middle of the terminal and took Meg in his arms. He didn't say anything. He just kissed her again and held her tightly.

They returned to the city the same way that Alan had left two hours before. Only this time the streets were alive. Soon after departing the Termini Centrale the number 64 bus was packed with passengers, and it did its usual lurch and weave through the streets past the Piazza de Venezia on the way to St. Peter's Square. Meg still operated on nervous energy. They got off the bus next to the square, and with Alan carrying the large Samsonite they began the climb up the Viale Vaticano to the convent. It was 9:45 a.m. and the sun was warming them.

"It's like summer," Meg said.

"It's always summer," Alan answered.

No gypsies bothered them as Alan and Meg trudged alongside the Vatican walls past the entrance to the Sistine Chapel, crossing the street to the palazzo-like convent at number 90. A nun responded to Alan's ring. Meg stayed in the background. The buzzer sounded and Alan pushed open the large bronze door. They entered a garden filled with blooming red azaleas, ascended some steps, and entered a foyer with a marble floor. They put down their bags and a little nun emerged from somewhere, recognized Alan, then disappeared.

"I told them you were coming," Alan said. Meg nodded, still a little confused.

Alan carried the bag down a long corridor, past the bathrooms and showers and into room 12. "Here it is."

Alan pushed open the tall wooden shutters, revealing a garden below, not facing the Sistine Chapel side of the building but looking towards the Janiculum Hill.

Twin beds separated by a night table were up against the wall. Alan lifted the night table and put it on the side of one of the beds. He pushed the two beds together.

"*Voilà*. A double." Alan pulled Meg onto the bed. "It's so great to see you. Thanks for coming."

"Thanks? For what? You couldn't have kept me away with wild horses."

Alan gave Meg a passionately long and hard kiss.

"Is it OK here?" she asked.

"Don't worry," Alan replied, "I think they know about the birds and the bees."

Rome hardly intimidated Meg. She relished the incessant traffic rushing along the Tiber, the parading herds of Spanish, French, or German tourists with guides holding up umbrellas or little triangular flags, the omnipresence of the camera-toting Japanese, the peal of bells that seemed to come from everywhere, and the city busses that belched black exhaust fumes. Like Mecca, New York, or Jerusalem, Rome was a tourist magnet for millions.

eight

10/2/78

Dear Kristin:

Rome is beautiful. The flight was fine; Dad met me at the airport and I was half asleep. So far we saw all the great sights to see here. The first day we took a bus tour of Rome to get a feel of how big the city is and its main places. Then we went back to the Colosseum, the Piazza España (my favorite), and the Forum. We have walked and walked. This aft we walked around the Jewish Ghetto and visited the synagogue. Tonite is our last night in Rome and we are going to Trastevere for dinner. A little trattoria not in the guidebooks. Your dad (the expert) says that the best food in Rome is in Trastevere. Every night we went for ice cream to the Piazza Navona. Your dad (the expert) says that the best ice cream in the world is in the Piazza Navona! I think he's right. Tomorrow we leave for Venice and Florence.

I love you and I am thinking of you constantly. Give Grandma and Vicky a big kiss for me.

MOM

nine

The express train for Venice was scheduled to leave Rome's central station at 7:30 a.m. Meg and Alan had overpacked so they left a box of clothes in the convent, making arrangements to pick them up when they returned to Rome for their one-night stay at 90 Viale Vaticano. Even though it was 7:00 a.m. when they arrived at the station, throngs of people were rushing to the subway, to the bus stops, or struggling with boxes and valises before getting on a train. The kiosks selling newspapers were doing a brisk business and the fruit stands were open.

The train was waiting on Track 22. People were climbing aboard. Meg and Alan were in Car 220, a second-class coach, seats 76 and 78. They struggled with their bags up the coach steps and searched for their seats.

"It's a compartment," Meg said, surprised.

Alan slid open the door. A young soldier in uniform sat in the corner. "*Buon Giorno*," he said.

"*Buon Giorno*," replied Alan. He hoisted the bags onto the ledge above the seats, and Meg and he settled into what seemed like easy chairs.

Soon the compartment filled. A nun, two children with their mother, and an older man added to the little family of travelers.

All of them may not have been going to Venice. The first stop was Firenze, then Bologna, Pisa, and Fiesole. The compartment's composition could change before Alan and Meg arrived at their final stop.

"Is this an express train?" Meg asked.

"It is. But express means something different than what we're used to," Alan answered. "It doesn't mean nonstop."

"It feels like the Orient Express."

"Well, it isn't."

Alan had been apprehensive. He was concerned first of all that they wouldn't arrive at the station on time, and second that there would be a mix-up in seats. Even though he could speak Italian, Alan knew it could be messy if he found someone sitting where they should be. Alan felt that the responsibility for making sure that the trip went smoothly rested on him. His fear, at least for the time being, was misplaced. They were seated on the right train, in the right coach, and in the right seats, on their way to Venice.

At exactly 7:30 the train began to move slowly out of the station and it arrived on time.

As soon as Meg stepped into the massive Piazza San Marco in Venice, she knew she was in a special place: the eleventh-century square surrounded on four sides by the Palazzo Ducale, the eighth-century Campanile, renaissance buildings and arcades, the famous Caffe Florian that opened for business in 1720, everything in the square seeming to converge on the Byzantine and grandiose Basilica di San Marco. Meg had been startled by the novelty of stepping off the train from Rome and into a waiting "water taxi" that zoomed her to the Pension Adelphia along a watery highway.

The canal boats were a faithful tableau of Venetian life: matrons with shopping bags filled with vegetables and the day's dinner, cargoes loaded and unloaded for the corner hardware store, schoolboys in gray trousers and starched white shirts and young girls in plaid skirts and white blouses with little red bows in their hair, riding on the water taxis as if they were riding on a local bus. And why not? This was their local bus!

On the afternoon of their arrival Meg and Alan went directly to the city's major attraction, St. Mark's Square.

"New York has its Times Square, London has Picadilly Circus, Paris the Place de la Concorde. Venice has this. And there are no cars!" Alan was talking to himself.

Meg thought about the pigeons. In college she had read Evelyn Waugh's *Brideshead Revisited* and she always remembered the beginning of the chapter that spoke of the pigeons of St. Mark's. "Memories flooded into Sebastian's mind like the pigeons of St. Mark's." And here they were in front of her; the plaza was thick with them, hundreds of them fluttering about, feeding off the corn that the tourists purchased from the women at the little trestle stalls.

Meg wandered through the square, absorbed in her thoughts even though hundreds of people mulled around. She marveled at the patterned floor of the plaza, the ledges of the Campanile, the majestic piazza space that was animated but dignified. Meg walked under the Ala Napoleonica which the former emperor built in the early 1800s when his troops occupied Venice. Then she passed the Procuratorie Vecchie with its shops. The Caffe Quadri was serving coffee to the tourists just as it had served Turkish coffee to Napoleon's troops. Meg lost herself in the romantic images of an era long past. She glanced down the Mercerie that led to the Rialto, then faced San Marco's again.

Alan was not far behind.

"You're right," Meg said. "Once you said that Venice was the only city in the world that you had to see with someone."

Their first night in Venice Alan and Meg ate at the *Osteria del Chiasso* but only after having a drink at Harry's New York Bar.

"You're kidding," was Meg's remark when Alan suggested they go to Harry's.

"No, it's great. You'll love it. It's right off the square. It's a Venice landmark."

"A Venice landmark?"

"Yeah. Really. It used to be for American tourists but it's not anymore. Come on."

So they went to Harry's. The Adelphia was about a half mile from St. Mark's over two stone bridges and through some narrow streets, but the evening was pleasant so they walked. Meg wore a little black dress and she put a sweater over her shoulders.

The bar was noisy.

The *Osteria* was more to Meg's liking.

After dinner they walked slowly hand in hand through St. Mark's Square. To the right of the basilica they could see the water lapping at the edge of the plaza. The moon was out. It was chilly. A little orchestra played at the entrance to the Florian. Alan took Meg and began to dance with her.

"When will we ever again have the chance to dance in the Piazza di San Marco?"

Meg rested her head on Alan's shoulder and closed her eyes.

People passing by paid no attention to the couple dancing in the square. It seemed to be the most natural thing in the world to do.

Next afternoon Alan and Meg were shopping for some Murano glassware to bring home as gifts. Alan got involved in choosing the correct shade of blue from a batch of pieces in a little store off one of the squares. Meg said that she was going up the street to see what she could find and would meet Alan in fifteen minutes in front of the shop they were in. When Alan finished he left the store and went outside to wait. Ten minutes passed, twenty, thirty, and still no Meg. Alan went up and down the confusing jumble of narrow streets, tried reading a map, but he didn't want to go too far from the place they said they would meet.

When evening came, the shopkeepers pulled the iron shutters over the store windows. Darkness fell and Alan began to worry. An hour and a half passed and still Meg didn't show up. Alan thought of going to the police. She might have returned to the pension but he had no way of knowing that. He was frightened that something terrible had happened.

Then she appeared, walking down the street towards him, crying. "I got lost. All the streets seemed the same and when they clanked the shutters down, I didn't know where I was."

Tears were falling. Alan was angry but relieved that she was safe. "I was just about ready to go to the police. Couldn't you just make the right turn back to where I was waiting?"

"I went the other way."

"Let's go back to the pension. I'm too upset to go anywhere tonight."

"It's our last night here. I'm really sorry. But I was scared too."

"Didn't you have the address or the card of the pension?"

"No."

"I'm hungry."

They stopped at a small pizzaria for a silent dinner.

The next morning they took the express train to Florence. Bad luck again. They found two seats on the crowded train. When the conductor collected their tickets, he told them they had to move because they were in a first-class section and their tickets were for second class. Alan pulled down the bags and they made their way to the second class coach. Soldiers occupied almost all of the seats. None were empty. Alan and Meg stood for two hours.

"Nice work. For getting us into the wrong coach."

"At least you sat down for an hour."

"We should've played dumb and not moved."

"Wouldn't work."

When the train stopped at Pisa, they got off and bought some fruit and three pieces of fresh bread and Mocego cheese.

The train arrived in Florence on time at 11:55 a.m.

ten

Castello di Uzanno
Firenze, Italia 09986
TEL 39-055-85032

10/11/1978

Dear Mom and Kristin,

I am writing this letter to you from one of the most beautiful places in all of Italy. We arrived in Florence from Venice the day before yesterday, but instead of staying in the city we are experiencing the rustic tranquility of the countryside. We live in a "Villa", the Castello di Uzanno, that really means an old farmhouse, about five miles from Florence. But it is gorgeous. We have a vineyard and a courtyard and gardens with lemon trees and even a pool. Our room has leather chairs and a featherbed with a down comforter. Ancient urns and statues dot the grounds and a restaurant occupies what used to be the house kitchen.

We are in Tuscany, gentle rolling hills, vineyards, stone farmhouses, umbrella pine trees, olive groves, fields of sunflowers, and the sun. No wonder Dante and Michelangelo were inspired here!

Yesterday we visited Florence and we saw the cathedral, built in 1296 (I sound like one of our tour guides), and next to it is the famous bell tower that is supposed to be the most beautiful in Italy. The painter Giotto drew up the plans in 1334. Long time ago and it's still standing!

Florence is packed with tourists even though the tourist season hasn't started yet. I think it has. But they don't bother me. The trip so far has been beautiful.

You would love the Old Bridge, the Ponte Vecchio. This bridge spans the Arno River on the edge of the city, and on it are a lot of shops and goldsmiths. Old tradition. The bridge doesn't have the charm of the Rialto in Venice, but it beats the Brooklyn Bridge.

We tramped and tramped yesterday. San Marco, the Duomo, the Ufizzi with its collection of renaissance paintings, the Medici Chapel, the Pitti Palace. Almost too much to take in in one day. We are off to Rome again tomorrow. I don't want to go, it's so beautiful here. But we will. I have been taking pictures like mad and I will go through all of them when I see you.

I miss you both very much. Dad has been a great tour guide. Grumpy sometimes but fun.

I hope that this letter doesn't arrive in Boston after I do. I'm sending it Special Delivery.

With all my love,

Mom

Part Three
Providence, RI

eleven

"Do you love your wife?"

At first Alan thought that he didn't hear what he knew he heard. The captain started to announce that the plane was over Providence, RI, just when the man in 6E turned and started to speak.

"Pardon me?"

"Do you love your wife?" the salesman repeated.

"With all due respect, that's a stupid question. Of course I do."

"Well, last week I was reading in a magazine that the reason we choose this mate rather than that one is because we think that we'll have stronger and healthier offspring."

Alan was dumbfounded.

"Nothing to do with love or anything like that. Just whether we'll have strong, healthy children."

"That sounds too much like the Nazis. Super race and that kind of stuff."

"Maybe. The guy who first started saying this was a German. Schopenhauer. You know, the God is Dead guy."

"That was Nietzsche."

"Whoever," said the salesman with a shrug of the shoulders.

"I think there's more to falling in love than imagining the result of copulation," was all that Alan could muster.

The man in 6E went on as though Alan hadn't said anything. "What really makes somebody fall in love? Or is there really

69

such a thing? Is a woman who's 35 or 40 pressing the emergency button when she says she's 'in love', or is she making herself believe that she's really in love with the guy? Or vice versa? Not so I think for the man. My brother advised me not to get married until I was 35. I didn't pay any attention. He was right."

Alan was overwhelmed. "You are confusing two different issues," Alan began philosophically. "One is the question of the nature of love. The other is the perceived need for a woman to get married. The man is not that concerned with 'getting married', while the woman is. Why?"

Alan threw out his own question as a way of replying to the ones raised by the man in 6E.

"Children," said the man in 6E. "Women see their *raison d'être* as motherhood, whether they're married or not."

"What about love? Where does that enter the equation?"

"It doesn't. See, Neitzsche was right."

"You mean Schopenhauer."

The pharmaceutical salesman settled back into his seat and Alan the professor now found himself on the other side of the desk.

Did he love Meg? How could he now say that he loved her after a deliciously sensuous weekend with Robyn? Was his betrayal of Meg a symptom of a love that was ending? Or had it already ended? Was his affair with Robyn a gift from whomever? A gift of something that he was not getting out of his marriage to Meg?

Or did he love Robyn too? Could he love two women at the same time? Absurd, even though his rationalizing side wanted him to believe it. But don't some people believe in having more than one wife? They love each of them, don't they? Or is there such a thing as "the premier wife", like George Orwell's pigs: "we're all equal, but some are more equal than others?"

The salesman succeeded in getting Alan to reflect on the

deeper side of his relationship with Robyn, at least for the moment, even though he never intended to. Was Alan in love with Robyn? Was he in love with Meg? Or was he in love with Alan? How could he put himself outside of the bonds that he had created between himself, Kristin, Meg, and Victoria? Could he be so selfish as to put his own personal happiness over theirs? "I don't care what happens to you. This makes me feel good. So I'll do it," following Ernest Hemingway's dictum, "If it feels good, do it." No matter what harm it causes to others.

twelve

"I *should* get married."

Was that the real reason why Alan asked Meg to marry him? Did he think it was something he *should* do? After all the hours he spent with her, captivated by the rhythms of her walk, her voice, her feelings, her lovemaking, her whole being? Was it simply time to get married? He was 34. All of his friends were either thinking of getting divorces or breaking off relationships, and he wanted to get married. Was it isolation? The feeling of being alone? Maybe he began a search for the magical experience, and he thought he had found it with Meg.

Alan closed his eyes, but the words love, eros, sex, and friendship kept turning over in his head. They had always been part of his psyche but he kept it deep within and when he resurrected them, it was always in the context of preparation for a class. The great lovers that Dante had relegated to the bowels of hell, Troilus and Cressida, so illustrated how love caused the greatest pleasure and the greatest hurt that they always found a place in Alan's lectures. But for Alan the nature of love was always somewhere out there, something at the end of a microscope, examined, analyzed, and dissected. It never was a conscious part of his own being. Now it was.

"Do you believe in love at first sight?"

It took Alan a second to realize that the pharmaceutical salesman was questioning him.

"No," he snapped. "Sounds romantic, but...."

"I'm not so sure," the salesman said. "A friend of mine met a girl at P.J. Clark's. You know, the bar on 51st and 2nd. As soon as he laid eyes on her, Wammo! That was it. He knew she was the one. They talked all night just like they knew each other from another world. He married her. Still married after twelve years."

"I don't know," Alan replied. "There are just as many stories about couples separating after a quickie." He continued. "I know a guy who used to go skiing in New Hampshire. He met a knockout in one of those apres-ski places. Blonde, tanned, great figure. She came on to him. Body language. The 'emotional' muscles. First kiss. Boom. Sparks flew. Married in a month. Two weeks later she left him. She wanted a divorce."

"So he didn't see what she was really like!"

"Exactly. How could you after a week? Sparks. Thunder. Chemistry. You don't see the flaws until it's too late."

"Everybody has flaws," the salesman said.

"Yeah, but to really pull your way through a marriage, you have to be aware of at least some of them. She's good in bed. So that's a reason to marry somebody? Unless you're willing to work on a relationship, it's doomed. Compromise, you have to compromise."

Alan closed his eyes, thinking the "love at first sight" discussion was over. He was wrong.

"I think it's in the eyes."

"What's in the eyes?"

"Did you ever look directly into a woman's eyes, say at a bar. And she kept staring back?"

"She wouldn't if she was with somebody. The three-second rule!"

"What's that?"

"If you're a guy, you can look at another woman for only three seconds, then your date gets mad."

"Good rule," the salesman said. "So if she's alone or with

another girl, she focuses on you. Like when tigers first meet. I saw two tigers on the TV show *Animal Planet*. They stared and stared at each other and kept circling each other."

"Why?" Alan asked.

"Looking for signs. Danger. Aggression. Harm. With us it's looking for signals of a snub. Whether the other person is going to give you a come-on, and then say, 'Gotcha,' or is he for real."

"Get off it," Alan laughed.

"No, I'm serious."

"Where did you hear that? Sounds like drugstore psychology, right out of one of those 'Perfect Happiness in 30 Seconds' books.

"I think that falling in love has two stages," Alan began. "The first is really passionate, when you fall for the girl and just want to sleep with her. You're all over her. Close, body to body. Can't wait to get her in bed. And she's the same. But that wears off, gradually. Then comes the hard part, a long-term commitment. Did you ever read anything by Gabriel García Márquez? The Colombian writer?

"No," answered the salesman.

"He wrote a book a few years ago with a crazy title, *Love in the Time of Cholera*. But he says something that really makes sense. The problems in a marriage are over the trivial stuff. How he squeezes the toothpaste, whether he leaves the seat up, if she's always late. The hard stuff doesn't usually happen. And if it does, it doesn't cause the serious problems."

"Serious problems?"

"Whether to separate. Or divorce. Or even take a break from the relationship. Most people don't know how to be alone. They *have* to be with somebody."

"Hey, that's pretty good. 'Take a break from the relationship.' " The pharmaceutical salesman looked up at the airplane ceiling, then at Alan.

"What happened to commitment?" he asked.

"It's still there," replied Alan. "On hold."

"Maybe the Indians have it right after all," the salesman said, looking at the ceiling again.

"How's that?"

"My friend Vidaya had her husband chosen for her."

"You mean in an arranged marriage?" Alan asked.

"Yep. And it worked. Vidaya's parents picked out the guy. Didn't let either set of hormones into the picture. Perfect objectivity."

"And that led to love?" Alan asked with some doubt in his voice.

"She says yes. The first time she held his hand. Or when he put the sash around her waist, she felt that special tingling. They ended up smitten with each other."

"They had to make it work, that's why. They wanted to make it work."

"Maybe the idea of romantic love is overblown," continued the salesman.

"Comes from the Middle Ages. They called it Courtly Love," Alan added. "The knight and his lady fair."

Alan closed his eyes and began to think about his courtship of Robyn. How they started to open up to each other during their morning runs. The man in 6E kept chattering but Alan wasn't listening.

One morning Alan had asked Robyn, "What about you? What brought you to Boston, from Iowa? Or Wisconsin? Someplace in the Middle West."

"How did you know I was from the Middle West?"

"Accent. You still have that Middle West intonation."

"I do? Who are you. Henry Higgins, you know, from *My Fair Lady*?"

"Nope. But the accent's still there. It's cute."

"Thanks."

75

"Soooo?"

"I was raised in Indianapolis. Or Indianoplace, as some people call it. Actually, outside of the city, closer to Bloomington. I went to Indiana U. Majored in Folklore."

"There's a major in that?"

"Sure. There's a major for everything. After graduating I went to New York City, the big city, for excitement, to find myself, you know, we were going to save the world, sing songs and hold hands. I lived in Woody Allen's New York, on the Upper West Side. Totally fake!"

"So where does Eric come in?"

"We met at Maxwell's Plum on Second Avenue. The bar scene was great in those days. No AIDS to worry about. We even slept together on our first date."

"Do you still sleep together?"

"I'm not going to answer that."

"Don't."

"He has lots of great qualities."

"Anyway. More about Robyn."

"Eric was doing his residency at Belleview Hospital on the East Side. We had a torrid romance. I fell in love, and then we moved to Boston."

"And lived happily ever after."

"Nope. The shine began to wear off after about a year. I began to get the feeling he was having an affair. But I was totally ignorant. One day he told me that one of the nurses he worked with had invited us for dinner at her place near Mass General. We went. Just after we arrived at her apartment, she said, 'Let's have a drink.' Eric jumped up and said, 'I'll get it.' It hit me like a ton of bricks. How did he know where the liquor was? She must have been sleeping with him right under my nose. The clincher came when I found a note she had written reminding him of lunch with Kat. Her name was Katherine. It was in the pocket of his pants I was taking to the dry cleaners.

I had Emily and imagined that the baby would pull us together. She didn't."

"So why do you think she invited you to dinner?"

"Maybe she wanted to size me up."

"So you're unhappy?"

"Actually, no. I've learned to live with ambiguity."

"Wow. Neat trick."

"It's like depression. Long periods of just keeping the whole thing out of my mind, then a sudden drop. The intervals in between get longer. Or I fantasize about going to Spain and living with my lover in a beach house. Blazing sun, blue water. What about you and Meg?"

Robyn was sincere. She didn't ask the question as a way to turn the discussion back on Alan.

"Meg's a great mom."

"I didn't ask that."

"I know. I'm thinking about an answer."

"I won't ask if you've ever had an affair."

"Don't. You might be surprised."

"So I'll lower it a notch. What about *your* sex life?
Alan laughed.

"Lower it? That's not lowering it. That's raising it."

"You asked me. So I'm asking you. Tit for tat."

"It dropped off," Alan said seriously, "about six years ago, maybe seven. Some time after we were married. I really don't remember when. The pleasure of a companion, I guess, was what really pushed me on originally. And when we had sex, the feeling lessened. I mean, we had sex not only less often, but with less feeling in it."

"That's funny. A friend of mine left her husband but they get together every so often, and she says the sex is still great!"

"Maybe she has no connect between the head and below the belt! I think there is."

"Was it Meg's fault or yours?"

77

"I don't know. I suppose if you ask her, it was my fault. Ask me, and it's hers."

Alan suddenly switched internal channels.

They took the "long" run that morning, around the park, across the bridge, then skirting the boat lake.

"My neck was too long," Robyn said. "I was really self-conscious as a kid. My classmates teased me and called me the swan. I hated them for it. So I always wore a turtle neck."

"Even in summer?"

"No. Not in the summer, silly."

Silly. That playful word let Alan know he had entered Robyn's space.

The trees around the perimeter of the lake were almost bare. But some had brown leaves ready to fall. The October morning air was clear and crisp.

She's another Hera, Alan thought, reaching into his Greek mythology bookcase to categorize the woman he began to run with in the mornings. Spouse, helpmate, chum, confidante, even assistant. She fit the role. At this point he never imagined an affair would result. He knew Robyn as a woman married to the doctor and psychologist, Eric Taylor. But Robyn didn't think of herself as the Greek goddess, Hera. Perhaps she fancied a more modern incarnation.

But who?

She's more like Aphrodite, Alan imagined. A charmer, seducer. Maybe even a lover. Alan's fantasy kept pace with the cadenced rustle of Robyn's pants legs brushing against each other. She wore a gray Gore-Tex outfit and Nike running shoes with a red band holding her hair down and even though it was a chilly October morning, Alan wore a T-shirt and shorts and anklets under his Sauconys.

"I really wanted to be accepted by my friends in the seventh grade," she continued.

"Don't we all at that age?" he blurted out.

"Yeah, but you have no idea how much I wanted to."

"High school was no different. And college was the same. I dropped out of Babson after two years."

A sudden lurch and the light went on telling the passengers to fasten their seat belts. The pilot came back on the loudspeaker.

"Folks, we're running into a little clear air turbulence. So keep your seat belts on for a few minutes till we get out of it. Just a few minutes."

Alan turned in his seat towards the man in 6E. The pharmaceutical salesman was reading *Forbes*.

"Hey. You're awake," he said, lowering the magazine.

"You know, what we were talking about before. Ever realize how many women say they were attracted to the guy because he made them laugh? You rarely hear that I was attracted because he was smart, or because he was kind."

Alan thought for a moment. "Doesn't Shakespeare say something in *Julius Caesar* about surrounding himself with fat people because they are jolly? But you do hear that the guy was physically attractive. So we're attracted by some 'special qualities' that the other one has?"

"Or we happen to be physically near the other person a lot of the time. Like at work, or in the same apartment building, or taking the same bus to work. You know what," continued the salesman, "I heard once that people who live near stairways, entrances, doorways where people are always going in and out, they have more friends than people who live in the same building but are not near the flow of traffic. *Brief Encounter*. Remember the old movie?"

Maybe the salesman was onto something.

"What about: Opposites Attract?" countered Alan.

"I never understood what that meant."

"It means," said Alan with a slightly patronizing tone, "that people seek friends who have some quality that they lack; that

79

will balance what they have. To fill the gap."

The salesman's face asked for an explanation.

"Like if the guy likes sports, or is really aggressive and dominant, he chooses a woman who is totally feminine, not necessarily who doesn't like Sunday afternoon football, but who is cheerful, sympathetic, warm, tender, nurturing. You know what I'm saying?"

Alan caught himself using the phrase he promised himself he would never use. How many times did he say to himself, 'Of course I understand what you're saying. I'm not stupid.'

"But that Opposites Attract theory has been debunked."

Alan was surprised. All he could muster was, "Really?"

"Sure. The happiest couples and those that stay together longest are those who are really well matched in education, common hobbies, ambitions, interests."

Alan said nothing. It made too much sense.

He began thinking that if he and Robyn didn't share a common interest in running, he wouldn't have beaten a path to New York City to meet her. In his case being at the same place, the park, at the same time, the morning, drew them together. Maybe if she lived in Cambridge or in another part of Boston, he wouldn't have been willing to go to the trouble of getting to know her.

"But don't you think that proximity, or familiarity, and that's what we're talking about, can also breed hostility? The opportunities for conflict and hostility increase."

"Sure, they can," said the salesman, "and sometimes they do."

In Alan and Robyn's case the opposite happened.

After the "long run," Alan took the plunge, a major step, of inviting Robyn to the Juicery, the kiosk in the park that had a few benches and tables scattered around it to have a drink, carrot juice, or strawberry juice, as long as it was organic and not artificially flavored. He intended to stay only long enough to chat for a few minutes but the minutes lasted a full hour. Alan couldn't even remember what they talked about. They parted with a wave—he to his car, she to hers.

thirteen

"Better if I call you," Robyn whispered to Alan.

The caveat surprised him. Perhaps she really knew how to begin an affair. They had just finished a morning jog and offhandedly Alan made the suggestion that someday they have lunch. Robyn had been kidding about how she loved Italian food, almost as if daring him to say, "Hey, I know a great place for Italian. Let's go sometime." He did. And he added, "I'll call you."

So one gloomy Thursday in November Alan and Robyn lunched at Carmen's, a romantic little restaurant, it seats only 28, in the North End, right next to the Paul Revere House. Alan had to get back to school for a committee meeting at three and Robyn had some shopping to do at Filene's, so it was convenient for both. Neither could dally. Alan was nervous. He was not having coffee with a co-ed in the college cafeteria discussing whether *Brunelleschi's Dome* deserved to be a best seller. The stakes were higher. But Alan enjoyed skating on the edge, taking the risk that imperiled the security of his marriage, and surely a lunchtime date with Robyn did. Did he see the woman in front of him as one who was restoring a self-image that he suspected was lost? He would never relinquish the security of marriage. Only risk it. Alan accepted his entrance into the dangerous age of infidelity confident that he would not succumb.

Their table at Carmen's was near the front door. Robyn

ordered grilled flatbread laden with caramelized onions, grapes, gorgonzola, and walnuts. Alan followed suit.

"Samers," she said.

"A bell-ringer. I haven't heard that word since I was a kid," Alan answered.

Robyn laughed.

"So how do you survive in class with all those nubile bodies in front of you?"

Alan was slightly embarrassed.

Robyn continued. "Did you see the movie *Mr. Holland's Opus*?"

"I did. But that was about high school. By the time kids get to college, they're into other things besides their teachers."

"Didn't you ever hear of sleeping your way to A's? Here, I'm telling you!"

"That's OK. I don't have all the answers."

"You're supposed to. You're the professor."

Alan's eyes kept going to Robyn's lapel pin, a silver angel, about an inch high, that contrasted with the dark gray jacket she wore. Dark blue pants matched her blue turtleneck.

"I like your pin."

"Angels are in, this year."

"When did you start running?"

"Oh, not too long ago, three, maybe four years."

They talked about the new contraption that Robyn saw in a running magazine, hard rubber clamps that hooked on to running shoes allowing you to jog over ice and snow; the Back Bay Fens Park, the advantages of living in Boston with all the music and theater and colleges in town.

Robyn was on the "offensive". She kept the conversation focused outside of herself, avoiding her interests. How she spent her days, her child, her family, and Eric, her husband, were never mentioned.

Alan remembered with meticulous exactness the details of

that first lunch at Carmen's. He recalled looking into Robyn's face, at the telltale tiny wrinkles beginning to spread from the corners of her eyes. Her light chocolate skin was clear, her dark, chestnut-colored eyes almost matching her dark brown hair. He wondered why she had brown eyes. He began to undress her, slowly, first her gray suitcoat, then her pants, her shirt, her bra. Then, he thought to himself, *Wait a minute.* He remembered Meg once saying, "There is nothing less sexy than a naked body. Takes away all the imagination. Better she have on that little black dress."

"Hey, where are you? You're not here."

"Yes I am."

"You're in another world."

"No. Not at all," Alan lied.

"So tell me, what's Meg like?"

Alan was surprised at the question. Not so much at the content but at the question's directness. Robyn never dwelt on her own husband or family, and now she asked him about his wife.

"Where did you meet her?"

"Oh my God, we were kids in grad school. At Boston U. Long, long time ago."

"It couldn't have been *that* long ago."

"Seems like ages."

"Classroom sweethearts?"

"Nothing that chaste. We met at a prof's party."

"That was chaste, I bet. In the seventies. Come on!"

Alan wasn't sure whether Robyn was being ironical or not. Or trying to be. Her voice didn't show anything but genuine interest in how he had met Meg.

"Hey. Look at the time. You don't want to be late."

Alan mumbled something about not starting until he got there. He paid the check, and both he and Robyn left the restaurant and walked toward the parking lot on Hester Street, a block away.

"It was nice."

"The food?"

"No, having lunch with you."

Robyn didn't reply.

When they reached the parking lot Robyn said, "Are you going to run tomorrow?"

"Yes."

"Me too. See you there."

She got into her black Honda Civic, looked up at Alan, and smiled.

"Don't forget," she said.

"I won't."

"And thanks for the lunch. It was nice."

He waved.

Robyn pulled out of the parking lot and headed up Commonwealth for Filene's. Alan stood for a minute, then he turned, found his own car, and started the drive back to school.

Oddly, he began to think about Meg and not about Robyn. He recalled the first fumbling kiss in the doorway of her flat in Brookline. After a few minutes she said, "We'd better go upstairs. Come on, I'll make some coffee." Meg started to make the coffee. But Alan came up behind her, put his arms around her waist, and she turned. They began to kiss again and ended up making passionate love on the kitchen floor. He had to help her to the couch. Or maybe she helped him. They stayed locked in each other's arms for what seemed like hours. Alan remembered that it was well past midnight when he left, making his way slowly down the creaking stairway, afraid that Meg's neighbors would hear him. After that night he found it hard to stay away. And when she was in his arms, he wondered when he would be able to stay all night and not have to creep away in the dark.

In two hours Alan was back at Salem State.

fourteen

"Thanks for the lunch yesterday. It was great."

"Oh, that's OK. I enjoyed it too, you know."

"Really?"

"Sure."

"You seemed a wee bit nervous."

"Not really. I just wanted to get back to school for that meeting at three."

"Did you make it?"

"Plenty of time."

"We have to do it again when you're not so rushed."

*

"Is that a new running outfit?"

"No, I've had it for ages. Haven't worn it much. I got it in New York a couple of years ago."

"How come?"

"How come what?"

"How come you haven't worn it?"

"I have, silly. You just never noticed."

"It's really smart looking."

"Thanks."

"In fact, you look lovely in it."

"Really? Now that's a complement. But how could I look lovely draped in this gray, dull, bulky, formless, uncomfortable-looking thing? Even this band almost hides my hair."

"Are you finished?"

"Yes."

"Easy. You're a pretty woman."

"Compliment number two. Thanks."

"You know how to take a complement. Sign of an adult."

"Really? So now I'm an adult?"

"Why are you repeating everything I say?"

"I'm not."

"Sure you are."

"Anyway, how's Meg?"

"Oh, she's OK. They asked her to teach a course next semester in Brookline."

"That's something new. Will she do it?"

"I think so."

"Why only 'think'?"

"She's busy. Kids, home, working at school. Kristin's a handful. She's almost 14 going on 25, so she knows all the answers to all the problems. You remember when you were that age."

"Yeah. I wish I didn't."

"She's going with Meg to visit her mother next weekend."

"Oh really. Where? North Carolina?"

"Yes. They're flying down."

"When are they leaving?"

"Friday night."

"So you'll be 'alone'?"

"Yeah, right."

"Guess what?"

"What?"

"I'll be 'alone' too. Eric is away this weekend. Final seminar meeting in New York."

"What's the course?"

"I think it has something to do with Policy Issues and

Mental Health. I don't know, something like that. Hey, idea.
Let's take a long run on Saturday."

"Great. In the afternoon. That'll give me a chance to catch
up on some schoolwork in the morning. OK?

"Deal."

*

"How's Eric these days?"

"Eric who?"

"Eric, your husband. There's only one Eric in your life, isn't
there?"

"Yep."

"So? How is he?"

"Why do you ask?"

"To learn more about that part of Robyn's life. That's why."

"He's fine. Spends lots of time at work in the clinic, and
what's left over with his books, and whatever."

"What kind of degree is he getting?"

"One of those weekend MBAs. They call them Executive
MBAs. He goes to Tulane three weekends a month, and two
weekends around here."

"New York's not around here."

"Well, it's closer than New Orleans."

"Sounds like all his time is taken up."

"Short-term loss, long-term gain, is the way he explained it
to me."

"Do you buy that?"

"Sure, why not?"

"What's the long-term gain?"

"Options. He'll be able to pick and choose where he wants
to practice."

"In the meantime, you're supposed to stay at home barefoot
and pregnant in the kitchen."

"That's not even funny."

"Wasn't meant to be."

"Hey, we all have our little things to contend with. Don't we?"

"Guess so. But that doesn't sound so little."

"It's not bad. I'm glad he's doing what he wants to do."

"But it really must limit the time you guys have together, doesn't it? Sorry, I didn't mean to be so inquisitive."

"That's OK. What did Meg do when you were getting your Ph.D.?"

"We were studying, and starving, together. No my-turn-your-turn game."

"How romantic."

"Are you kidding?"

"No, I mean it."

"It wasn't romantic at all. I was glad it was over when we graduated and got jobs."

"Didn't you guys live together in a garret room with a candle flickering while you read together at night?"

"Now I know you're kidding."

*

"Are those new shorts?"

"They are. I bought three pair. Green, yellow, and these black ones. Do you like them?

"They're nice. That kind of material keeps you cool in the summer. Where'd you get them?

"At Fleet Foot, the new running store on Boyleston. I saw a really nice pair of Aspics, but the salesman said they weren't for me. I don't roll up enough weekly miles to warrant getting them."

"You look so chic. You're the only runner I know that can make a fashion statement at 7 o'clock in the morning."

"Who cares what you wear?"

"You do, obviously."

"What do you mean by that?"

"That you are careful about how you look."

"So? Isn't every woman?"

"Or man. I think guy runners are just as conscious about how they look. Or aren't you that observant?"

"Of course I am. I see your eyes popping sometimes."

"*Moi*? Never."

"Yeah, right."

fifteen

The drone of the plane was in the distance, far away. But not so far that Alan couldn't hear it.

"Dad, you're not putting it in the right way. Here, let me do it."

Kristin took the video out of Alan's hands and began to insert it into the VCR player. When she finished, she rolled her eyes as if to say that he was helpless, of no use. Even a child could do it.

"I didn't grow up in a video arcade," Alan remarked.

"Neither did I," Vicky retorted.

Meg was at a parent-teachers meeting and after the Friday night pizza, Alan, Kristin, and Vicky were going to watch the 1970s version of *The Three Musketeers*. Alan of course wanted to see Raquel Welch and the girls were just as anxious to devour Michael York.

"Dad, you running tomorrow?" Kristin asked unexpectedly.

"I dunno," he answered. "Why?"

"Well, Missy Fox asked me to meet her in Back Bay Fens Park tomorrow. She wants to go out for the cross country team and she has to practice, she says. Can you drop me off?"

"What time?"

"9:30, 10. Is that possible?"

Alan had told Robyn that he would meet her at ten and he really didn't want Kristin to see him with her. He didn't want to have to go through a song and dance about "my friend" the runner, even though nothing, absolutely nothing, was going on.

"Call Missy and make sure she's going. I don't want to get there to find out she stiffed you."

"OK. I'll call her later."

"Better now."

"OK."

Kristin jumped up from the couch and went into the foyer to make the call.

Alan was stalling for time, or maybe even a reprieve. Perhaps Missy wasn't going and so Kristin wouldn't go either.

Alan could hear Kristin talking above the movie trailers. Then she came back.

"Never mind. She's not going."

For a split second Alan wondered whether Kristin would ask to go anyway. She didn't and Alan didn't suggest she join him. But Vicky did.

"Why don't you go anyway, Kristin?" Vicky teased.

Vicky knew that Kristin didn't enjoy running, so Alan was taken aback when she asked about going to the park.

Alan remained silent after Vicky's remark.

Then he mumbled, "Let's watch the movie, OK?"

A mild deception? Or was it so mild? Alan pinpointed the episode as the first in a series of little deceits. But by a twist of logic, Alan didn't view them at the time as deceits.

"Men have a different approach to the male-female relationship," he remembered a friend saying once. The comment stuck.

"I wasn't being deceitful. The whole thing would have just confused Kristin. Keep her out of it. She wouldn't understand."

Understand what?

sixteen

"You must have had a late night?"

"Not really. I'm tired. Got up early to make the plane."

Alan spoke to the salesman in 6E like he was an old friend.

"You were dozing."

"Thinking."

"Really? With your eyes closed?"

"Best way. Keeps out the distractions."

"Pleasant thoughts or not so pleasant?"

Alan didn't answer. He looked like the contented kitten that had just swallowed the family goldfish, eyes closed slowly drifting away from the salesman.

"You didn't tell me it was so big."

"It's not that big," with Meg dragging out the word, "that."

It was Alan's first inkling about the importance that Meg put on owning a house. Not an apartment, nor one floor of a double.

"I don't want to be somebody's janitor. I want someplace to call my own," was the way she put it. As if a three-story Queen Ann Victorian could be the only place to call your own.

Perhaps, Alan thought, he was totally, thoroughly mistaken. For Meg, a house was a refuge, a protection, a haven, a shelter, a fortress. Whoever or whatever was out there could huff and puff but never blow it down. Alan thought it was a waste to sink all that money into a bottomless pit of a house. It was not only ostentatious, it was impractical. At their stage in life a double would more than have sufficed. Meg didn't see it that way. So in Alan's mind she became a spendthrift. And in Meg's mind, Alan was insensitive to the deeper needs of a lifetime partnership.

"You're making me feel stupid."

"What?"

"You are. You're making me think that I'm the one who wants a big house that we can't afford. Well, we can afford it."

"No, we can't."

"My salary is $47,500 and yours is $36,500. Add them up!"

"We're in Boston."

"So?"

But they purchased the house, and it turned out not to be the bottomless pit that Alan imagined. In fact, Alan found a certain attraction to the old place, refinishing the Victorian staircase, and scraping the milk paint off the woodwork. But neither could quite overcome the original feelings about the other that surfaced when they had discussed the purchase.

Alan's interior video shifted swiftly to the park. He was running alongside Robyn.

They had chosen to run in the cross country section of the park even though the danger of turning an ankle in a rut or hole was increased.

"Do you always run in the morning?" Alan asked.

"Usually," Robyn answered.

"Why?"

"The rest of my day is too crowded. Experience taught me that you have to have a fixed time to exercise, otherwise you don't do it."

"Put it into your routine."

"Yep."

"Sounds addictive."

"It is."

"So, is that bad?"

"Not if it's a good addiction."

Although Alan couldn't pinpoint a precise date, he remembered that run in the park as the time when it first dawned on him how intensely attracted he was to Robyn.

"What do you know about addictions?"

"Oh. Enough."

"Like?"

"Like there are some you stay away from and some you accept as natural. And good."

Alan added good like it was an afterthought.

"So is running for you a good addiction or a bad one?"

"It's good, of course."

"Even with me?"

Alan turned his head without breaking stride and looked right into Robyn's eyes. "Of course, even with you."

For a few minutes the only sound that each heard was the soft pounding of running shoes on the cross country trail. Finally Alan said something. "I've been meaning to ask you."

"What?"

"Where's Casco? I never see him with you."

"Oh, he's around. The park's too strenuous for him in the summer. I take him for short walks around the neighborhood."

"Sounds like Rufus."

seventeen

In July of 1987 Alan and Meg rented a place on the Cape in Chatham. It overlooked the ocean near the lighthouse and the steps along the cliff side down to the beach provided a daily adventure for Kristin and Vicky. Alan had brought along his Sauconys but the crowds on the main streets made jogging almost impossible. Chatham was getting too touristy and he wasn't familiar enough with the side streets even for exploration runs. Alan finally found a route that took him past the Old Wharf, where you could buy fresh fish and up the wide street along the oceanside that originally had two big hotels that turned themselves into Conference Centers so that Boston's business people could patronize them all year round.

Alan had told Robyn that he was leaving for a "family" vacation. She joked about Chevy Chase's classic movie *Vacation.*

"Don't turn into a Clark Griswold, leading your clan to the Wally World Amusement Park."

"Why not? Some of his adventures were picaresque."

"No, they weren't. They were ambiguous."

Alan remembered the banter, not so much for the details, but for the disappointment that he sensed behind Robyn's jokes. He was going to be gone for at least two weeks. The "family" vacation declared that Alan belonged to others. His wife and daughters had first call on his time and his life.

On Tuesday, July 14th, it began raining around 3 o'clock in the afternoon. They had spent the morning at the beach, and even managed to eat the ham and cheese sandwiches that Meg prepared for lunch. But by two the dark clouds came rolling in and the predicted thunderstorm began. The thunderclaps rattled the two-bedroom cabin and the lightning flashed directly overhead. Kristin, Vicky, and Meg played Monopoly while Alan appeared engrossed in *The Bourne Identity* and writing an occasional postcard.

"Reading mysteries improves my writing style," he once said. "The details are vivid."

"When can we go to Provincetown?" Kristin asked.

"Not today," Meg replied. "It's an all-day outing. Tomorrow or Friday."

By 4 o'clock the rain stopped, the sun broke through, and they all went down to the Old Wharf to watch the fishing boats unload and to buy fresh fillet of sole for dinner.

Kristin and Vicky said they would prepare dinner, so Alan and Meg went for a walk on the beach.

"Remember when we came to the Cape after Daniel died?"

"Didn't we go to Truro?"

"I think so."

"We talked and talked."

"About what?"

"I don't know. What did anybody talk about in those days?"

"It wasn't that long ago. You make it seem like it was a century."

"Feels like it."

"I think it was during those talks when I really fell in love with you."

"Really. How come?"

"You seemed so cool. Almost a know-it-all. You were cute too."

"Were?"

"Even though your ears stuck out. Like Alfred E. Neuman."

"They did not."

"Yes, they did.

"So it wasn't just my gorgeous body you fell for?"

"Hey. Not only your brain."

"What else?"

"Ah ha, to the heart of the matter."

"We enjoyed each other. Didn't we?"

"I liked your cool interests. You know, jazz, literature, art, wine. And you really knew how to push my female buttons. You know, you were a great lover."

"Were?"

"Again?"

"What?"

"Remember long time ago, when were met at Prof. Lougran's house. You insisted that I take the leftover crackers and cheese home with me? And I said OK. Well, I hated leftover, soggy, crackers, and I still do. I threw them away as soon as I got home."

"You did?"

"Yes. You were so intent that I take them. I didn't want to say no."

"So, why did you?"

"You seemed so overbearing. Like you were looking down on me and my poor little Ed Psych dissertation."

"I was not."

"Well, I thought you were."

"I can't believe after all these years."

"And what really bothered me was your moving in with me in Brookline."

"How come?"

"I used the old apartment to decompress after work, alone. I needed my 'personal space'. In Brookline, I had to share it. I didn't know what to expect. I thought that even Daniel was unhappy. He urinated on the carpet."

98

"Upset?"

"Probably. If it was my place, I would have cleaned it up and forgotten it. But I didn't. The place was yours too."

Meg wanted an affirmation of what she was saying. She wanted Alan to say yes, they did have good times together. As though it was all in the past and the bad things could never happen again. As though her prior happiness provided the sustenance she needed today.

"I made believe I liked sports too."

"You *did* like sports."

"No, I didn't. I had the queer notion that I had to be lock-step with you in everything. Like what you liked. Hate what you hated. Do what you wanted."

"That didn't last long."

"Nope. We took different directions. Different interests."

"That saved us."

"That brought new energy to our 'relationship'. So I could talk to you about things that you had no interest in."

"Energy? Were you in Sidona? That sounds so California."

Meg continued more seriously, "You were the first and only one to listen to my daily depressions. What seemed so important to me then."

"But you weren't totally open."

"Of course not. Everybody has a little corner they keep to themselves."

"Go no further. I don't want to hear."

"Why not?"

"Let's go back. I smell the fish cooking."

The before-dinner walks on the beach became a vacation fixture for Meg and Alan. They reminisced, joked, held hands.

"If you weren't home, I felt like there was a big gap in the day."

"You always called."

"Sometimes I didn't."

"Did you get jealous? Thinking maybe I was with somebody else?"

"No I didn't. I figured you were at the library."

"They were hard days. But fun too."

"It was tougher when the kids came."

"Too many raised voices in the house. More than I wanted."

"How could you raise children, not have a 'real' job, and love a wife?"

"I could have done more, I think."

"How's that?"

"Oh, I don't know. Maybe I admired your inner strength, your self-discipline."

The afternoon walks in Chatham opened a channel between Meg and Alan, but it seemed that they were repeating a rehearsed script, a routine that Alan, at least, had heard before.

On the other hand, the separation from Robyn both satisfied and aroused Alan. He was the faithful husband and father, spending two weeks exclusively with his family. Sunbathing, making lunch, picking out the lobster and fish at the Old Wharf, walking in town, every activity had them and him enjoying each other's company. But when Kristin and Vicky finally went to sleep at night and Meg had turned over facing the wall on the other side of the bed, Alan began to think more about Robyn than the events of the day or what tomorrow would bring.

eighteen

In every sense Provincetown is as far out as the Cape gets. Here the prim shingled cottages and sedate New England greens one associates with the traditional Cape have been transformed into an entirely different style, with carnival overtones. Surrounded by peaceful dunes under the protectorate of the Cape Cod National Seashore, this long, narrow, harbor-hugging port at the tip of the Cape is a three-mile stretch of lively restaurants, galleries, and shops. In summer the population swells tenfold, from about 4,000 to over 40,000, and it may seem that every last visitor is strolling Commercial Street from daybreak until sometime after midnight.

When Vicky shouted, "Let's go," Alan looked up from the guidebook.

Meg was still in the kitchen putting dishes and forks away after breakfast and Kristin was out in the yard. They had halfheartedly agreed to visit Provincetown sometime during their stay in Chatham, maybe on a cloudy or rainy day, but there were none so today seemed as good as any.

Everyone piled into the rented Ford station wagon, they would eat lunch at Provincetown, and headed up Route 28 past Orleans, hitting Highway 6 just before reaching Eastham. Wellfleet and Truro sped past and in an hour they were driving by Kevin Shea's Watermark Inn on Commercial Street.

Provincetown was everything the guidebook said it was going to be. The shops, restaurants and old houses were almost too much to take in. Even the walk along the McMillan wharf was a thrill. But the hits of the day were the Whydah Museum, where Kristin and Vicky actually saw Pieces-of-Eight from the ship wrecked off Wellfleet in 1717, and the girls were enthralled with the idea that Provincetown, so out of the way and up the Cape Cod coast, was originally a haven for the outcast and the rebel. Somehow that struck a cord. When lunchtime came, the girls insisted on going to Napi's to indulge in Double Fudge Madness.

"Let's have lunch there," Vicky said.

"It's just a hotel," Alan answered. "There's plenty of other places around."

"Look at that place."

Meg was just able to make out the writing on the sign. "The Martin House," she drawled.

"Looks pricy."

"Three dollar signs. It is," Meg said, looking up from the Provincetown guidebook she had brought along.

"Never mind," Alan said, "we're on vacation."

"You and Mom go," piped up Vicky.

"We'll wander around and grab something someplace else."

Alan thought it was OK. Meg approved.

"Let's meet at the big lighthouse out on the wharf in two hours. Where the whale watching ship is."

They all agreed so Kristin and Vicky went exploring and Meg and Alan went into The Martin House for lunch. Almost immediately after they were seated, a waitress approached their table. She was a college student, probably from Boston down for the summer. About twenty years old, tanned, slim, with thin streaks of darker hair running through the blond that was pulled back in a bun. Khaki shorts and a black T-shirt.

She looked at Meg. "Something to drink?"

"I'll have a ginger ale, no, a root beer."

She looked at Alan.

"Diet something," he said.

"Pepsi OK?"

"Sure."

"Be right back."

There was something about the waitress that piqued Meg's antennae. The way Alan looked at her made her even more cautious.

She returned with the drinks.

"How's business?" Alan said to her.

"Great," she replied. "As long as you guys keep coming in."

She held the tray behind her back while she kept talking to Alan.

Meg sensed that Alan was totally at ease with her, perhaps because he was so familiar with females her age. But Meg also sensed that the young lady was playing the coy flirt and Alan loved the game.

"What brings you to Provincetown?"

"Why does anyone come?"

She took their order and in ten minutes returned with two thick Reuben sandwiches.

"Boy, that was fast."

"No faster than you deserve."

"Do you work here all year round?"

"Just for the summer. I'm studying at B.U."

"Oh, really. What's your major?"

"History."

"History? That's a weird choice, isn't it?"

"Not at all. I've always loved history."

"I mean, what can you do with a history degree?"

"I can paper my walls with it."

Alan and the young blonde laughed.

Meg detected an unseen language being spoken in her presence, one that went beyond a merely mild flirtation.

They finished lunch, met the girls and returned to Chatham.

nineteen

Ms. Robyn Taylor
3678 Essex
Boston, MA 32156

8/14/1987

Dear Robyn:

   Thought I'd drop you this card from Chatham to let you know that I miss the running every morning. *Correction:* I miss the running with *Robyn* every morning. The weather here has been wonderful. Just a couple of clouds and we did have a heavy downpour today. But all in all, the weather has cooperated and Clark Griswold has managed to stay out of trouble. How boring! But the Wally World Amusement Park is offering all the sights and sounds that one can imagine. Whatever that means!

   Hope you're staying in shape. See ya soon,

Alan

twenty

School began for Alan soon after he returned from the Cape. Actual classes didn't start until the last Monday in August, but he had to make sure that the college store had received the books he ordered, and he was always curious about who had signed up for his classes. Meg began work a little later but on her fell the burden of making sure that Kristin and Vicky had the cool clothes and the classroom tools they needed to begin school again.

But the start of this school year was a little different for Alan. He knew that he was going to spend the second week of October in Madrid at the Conference of Medieval Studies sponsored by the *grande dame* of European libraries, the *Biblioteca Nacional* of Spain. He had been to Spain only briefly in the seventies so he was looking forward to the trip. Meg wasn't going. Salem State was providing the lion's share of the costs because he was delivering a paper on Dante's role in the spread of vernacular Italian.

"What happens to your classes while you're gone?" Robyn asked.

"They'll survive. Test. T.A. More than enough to occupy the three hours."

"Wow. You're lucky."

"How do you mean?"

"How many of us have the luxury of just 'taking off'?"

"I'm not just 'taking off'."

"Oh, no?"

"No."

Alan was defensive. They ran in silence for a while.

Then Robyn said, "Can I go too?"

If Robyn had been watching, she would have seen Alan's face stiffen. The question took him totally by surprise.

"What would Eric say?" he finally blurted out.

"Probably get mad. What about Meg?"

"She'd think we were having an affair."

"Think?"

twenty-one

"People don't choose partners because they want healthy children."

It took a second for the salesman to realize that Alan was talking to him.

"I don't think so either," the man in 6E said, "but that's what some of the gurus think."

"They're wrong."

Alan was used to critiquing other people's ideas, and the German philosopher was simply one more target to aim at. He pulled out all the academic stops.

"It seems to me," he began, "that the evolutionary psychologists who believe that romantic love exists solely to improve human reproductive strategies base their ideas on the existence of an unrestrainable passion that creates a bond with somebody else. The early stages of passion, infatuation, bliss, exhilaration, are clearly associated with the increased levels of phenylethylamine in the body. Simply put, it's a short-term strong sex urge. But this explanation ignores one simple fact."

"Which is?"

"People want to go out of themselves, to go beyond their ordinary lives into another realm. Romantic love is not just driven by an urge to reproduce. One body is identified with another body. One body becomes the other body. There's the element of transcendence here."

"Dangerous."

"Why?"

"Because what you're saying is that this intense attraction involves an 'idealization' of the other. Into something the other might not be."

"Right. You're absolutely right."

The man in 6E settled back for a moment. Like he was getting ready for the next round. He said almost to himself, "But the woman can have an affair just as easily as the man."

Alan perked up. "What do you mean, affair?"

"You know, an illicit love affair. She's supposed to be with the girls on Thursday afternoon, not screwing some guy in a hotel room."

"It's usually the guy who's catting around, not the girl."

"Guess what?" the salesman said. "Recent theory."

"Oh, oh. Here it comes."

"Not if you think that four Ph.D.s from the University of New Mexico means drugstore psychology. They discovered that there's a connect between women's fertility periods and having affairs."

"Right out of Jean Auel."

"Exactly," laughed the salesman. "They start wearing skirts or dresses that look like they've been sprayed on, or they use a come-hither look with other guys, not their husbands, mind you, because, and get this, the kids would have different genes and not die off from the same disease all at once."

"Where did you see this gem?"

"*The Economist.*"

"*The Economist*? Since when does *The Economist* carry articles about reproductive strategies?"

"June 17, 1984."

"Women are more sexually aware—"

"Aware?" interrupted Alan.

"Yeah. Like they know what's going on inside them. They sense it. They're more aware when they're ovulating."

109

"So? What happens?"

"Well, they dress in sexier clothes. And they're more aggressive to men. But, and this is the interesting part, not to their husbands but to other men. They want to sleep with and get pregnant from the other guy."

Alan shook his head slowly.

"Men are just the opposite," continued the salesman. "They're afraid of getting the girl pregnant. So they avoid her if there's a risk of pregnancy. And these guys found that it didn't matter if the relationship was a solid one or whether he was a good provider or good in bed. The wives were really ready for a good roll in the hay, with somebody else."

"Maybe they were just bored. Or the guy was inadequate."

"No. These women's husbands and families were great."

"Something's missing," was Alan's only comment.

He knew that women were just as likely to cheat on their husbands as men on their wives, and they did because they could. Women were able to arrange a lunch or dinner, or even a hotel room, with a lover because they had the money and opportunity to do so, not like thirty years ago, when it would have been almost impossible. Work place affairs abounded, because the marriage was old and tired, or maybe it gave her more self-esteem, someone really cared about her, and she didn't have to talk baby talk, or maybe the unanticipated affair was just what she needed. There were a million reasons why the woman was just as likely to cheat, and feel absolutely no guilt! Researchers from New Mexico didn't have to tell Alan that.

Alan's eyes were closing again. He had braced when the salesman used the words "affair" and "hotel room" and "sexy clothing." He recalled Room 612 at the Gramercy Park Hotel, and Robyn's short, hunter green skirt, the one she wore to *Il Fiorentino's*. Was she trying to get pregnant?

The word "family" made Alan think of the Saturday

morning in late September when Kristin was scheduled for the final choral rehearsal for *The King and I*. She had worked all summer memorizing the lyrics and singing them in the shower, even setting up a make-shift stage in the basement to get used to being up front. Kristin was embarrassed to perform anything in public and she usually showed it by hunching over her shoulders with an expression that said she wanted to be elsewhere. But this time it was different. Kristin was thirteen and she took to heart what Meg had kept telling her about how important it was to acquire a sense of self-confidence and how it would serve her in high school and college, to say nothing about the business world. Alan promised to bring her to school around noon. The rehearsal was scheduled for 1 p.m. But Alan had gone to the Back Bay Fens Park for a Saturday morning run with Robyn, leaving the house with a wave and a shout that he would be back in time to take Kristin. He wasn't.

"Do you ever think of going back to work?"

"Never."

"Why not?"

"The question is why should I? I feel perfectly 'fulfilled', to use a current word, doing what I am doing."

"Which is?"

"Bringing up my daughter, being there for her when she comes home from school, helping her with her homework, going to PT meetings. I'm a concerned mother, as they say."

"What about your own growth. You working on that? Sorry. I didn't mean to prod. But I have a few moms in class who decided to go back to school and get a degree, in anything. They're different from the seventeen-year-olds who are majoring in landing a husband."

"How so different?"

"More serious about learning. They really want to be there. For the others, college is a holding center to keep youth off the labor market."

"That's not my field. You should know."

"Wish I did."

"Aw, poor Alan. You sound discouraged."

Alan looked at Robyn, not knowing whether she meant what she said or was teasing him.

In that instant Alan's left heel came down on a diamond-shaped stone that was large enough to twist his ankle and force him to slow up and start limping and moaning.

"What's the matter?" Robyn asked.

"Damn. I stepped on something. My ankle."

Alan did what he shouldn't have. He sat down on the side of the path and began to rub his left foot. Robyn leaned over him, looking while he pulled off his shoe and white running sock.

"Nothing broken. Stay here for a while and then start walking."

"OK."

After a few minutes, Alan got up, and putting his arm around Robyn's shoulder, began to walk, slowly.

"So much for the ecstasy of running," Robyn quipped.

Alan smiled.

"You OK?"

"Fine. But I still want to keep my arm around you."

Robyn tried to think of something ambiguously funny to say. She couldn't. Instead, she put her arm around Alan's waist.

"You need all the support you can get. Let's get some coffee."

At home, Meg and Kristin waited. Finally, a few minutes after 1 p.m. Meg took Kristin to her rehearsal, knowing she would be late for her own 1 o'clock curriculum committee meeting. Alan returned to an empty house.

"It wasn't my fault."

"You knew how important it was to her. Why did you even have to go?"

"I never imagined I'd fall."

"What about a little foresight? Anything, anything can happen. You know that."

"I'm sorry. Isn't that enough?"

"No. It isn't."

"Well, what do you want from me?"

"This damn obsession with running is driving me crazy."

"Why are you so annoyed that I'm doing something I enjoy?"

"You enjoy at our expense."

"Why don't *you* go out and do something?"

"Do something? All *you* have to do is take your daughter to a rehearsal. And you don't do it. You have to run. Every day."

Alan never saw Meg so upset. As far as he was concerned, he had left the house that morning with the intention of returning in time to take Kristin to her rehearsal. He wasn't trying to deceive anybody. Maybe he did stay a little too long at the kiosk resting his ankle and having coffee with Robyn. But it wasn't his fault that his heel came down on the stone the wrong way. It was unfair to blame him. Nor did Meg understand the running. It wasn't for rest or for play. When Alan ran, all the sticky complexities of family and work and their attendant obligations left him. He concentrated only on overcoming the physical demands that his running presented. The medieval scholars were probably right. For them, reading and study should take place while walking. The blood flowed more rapidly to the brain, they thought. For Alan, running was not only for exercise and fitness.

It enabled him, he thought, to think more clearly, to be more emotionally stable and resolute. Meg didn't understand this and Alan never tried to explain it. He thought of Ernest Hemingway's wife's remark. She once described the novelist's writing as an enticing prostitute, a rival who always seemed to have first call on his passions. Alan felt that his running was like Hemingway's prostitute.

twenty-two

October 11th came quickly. In the preceding weeks, Alan made sure that he didn't talk too much about Spain so that Meg wouldn't be too resentful of his European trip.

Meg, Kristin, and Vicky went to Logan Airport to see him off. Iberia Airlines Flight 42 nonstop to Madrid left on time at 7:10 p.m. As the 747 climbed higher, Alan glimpsed the fading lights of Boston on his left and he remembered Elton John's song about "Daniel My Brother" who took the plane to Spain and the red tail lights slowly faded as the plane climbed higher and higher into the sky. Alan thought about Meg and Kristin and Vicky. They had been excited because they sensed his excitement. They made him promise to send them postcards, even though they knew he would return before they arrived. Alan kissed Meg tenderly and hugged each of the girls. He waved and disappeared into the International Flight waiting room. Alan also thought about Robyn and the what-ifs surrounding her. What if he had arranged to meet her in Madrid? What if they did have dinner on the Castellana in one of the outdoor restaurants that dotted the old part of the city? What if they took a bus tour through the Guadarrama Mountains, visiting the places that Hemingway made famous in *For Whom the Bell Tolls*, and stayed in the old *parador* of San Lorenzo del Escorial? What if? What if? Alan closed his eyes to shut out the flurry of fantasies. But he couldn't get rid of them. He tried to sleep after dinner was served and the

114

movie was on, but he couldn't. So when the plane landed at
Barajas at 6 a.m. Madrid time, Alan was tired.

He showed his passport to the Guardia Civil at immigration,
had it stamped, picked up his Tourister hard top from the
baggage claim area, stumbled through customs, and made his
way to the bus that would take him to the Plaza de Colón,
which was near his hotel and also near the *Biblioteca Nacional*,
where the Dante meetings were going to be held.

AMBASSADOR HOTEL
Calle de Sagasta 34
Madrid

October 4, 1987

Dear Meg:

Here I am in Madrid. My third day here and so
far it has been fine. No major problems. The trip
over was great. That is, uneventful. Keep the bar
low so if there are no disasters, it's a roaring
success. Maybe I should raise it a little.

There was a couple next to me on the plane,
newlyweds I think, that were going to Madrid on
their honeymoon. Giggling and snuggling up to
each other all the way. Did we ever honeymoon?
Guess we were too busy then for that sort of thing.
Maybe we should think of a SECOND honeymoon.

Anyway, I was really tired after the trip. The bus
left me at the Plaza de Colón, which is just down

---

the block from the Ambassador Hotel, where I and several others attending the conference are staying. But it's uphill, up the Calle de Genova to a pretty plaza called the Plaza Alonso Martínez. There's a subway stop there so it's convenient. It's a neat hotel. All business. Small foyer, clean as a whistle, English spoken at the front desk. I have Room 412, sharing it with a professor from Wisconsin.

I was able to see the city for a bit on Sunday afternoon, that is, the day I arrived. Lots of people walking around and the sun was shining. I expected a chilly October day but it was more like the end of summer. Blue sky, not a cloud around. Now I know why they sang "the rain in Spain stays mainly on the plain." I walked all the way down to the Prado Museum but I didn't go in. No admittance charge on Sundays so it was mobbed. But I have to visit it sometime. You can't stay in Madrid and not go to the Prado. I'll just have to steal away sometime and indulge myself.

The old part of the city is centered around the square that has Philip II's statue in the middle, the Plaza Mayor. The entrances to the square are many and most of them are lined with *tapas* bars. They're great. All kinds of snacks before dinner, mainly seafood, and they eat late here, around 10 in the evening. Old Madrid is just to the left of the Plaza Mayor, between the plaza and the massive

Royal Palace. The streets are so narrow, the cars have to squeeze by. One of the fine old restaurants around here is the Sobrina de Botín. Specialty is roast suckling pig, or plain old pork. But the atmosphere is great. You have to bend your head to get into some of the nooks and crannies of the restaurant. Hemingway ate here and other luminaries. Touristy but nice. Next door is a must. The Arco de Cuchilleros, where they have flamenco dancing lasting to 4 or 5 in the morning. Sensual, loud, and it has to be accompanied by swigs of cognac. Interested?

Nothing like Italy though. Will write again soon. Love to Kristin and Vicky and *You* of course,

ALAN

AMBASSADOR HOTEL
Calle de Segasta 34
Madrid

October 5, 1987

Dear Robyn:

Here I am in the country of Don Quixote. I'm sure there are jogging places around but so far the only place that seems OK is the Parque del Moro, which is on the other side of the huge Palace of the Bourbon kings. Too much trouble getting there. I don't see anyone running in the streets here. The car is king. Maybe I'll just have to wait to get back to Boston for my daily runs.

I thought a lot about your question "Can I come?" Did you really mean it? Or were you just playing? How would we have ever managed to swing that one? Or are you laying down the line in the sand? Let's not rush things. I think we have a lot to talk about. Or is the talking time over. Time for Action! I feel different when I'm away from it all, the children, the wife, family obligations, school. It's hard to explain that "difference." Lonelier? Or is that too strong a word? I'm mixing things up. Anyway, Robyn, you have no idea how wonderful it is to talk with you about everything and let it all hang out, as it were. But anyway, I think that what we have together is more than a one-way street, you helping me. A shrink can do that. It's much more and I want you to know that. I wish you were here to answer and respond and get back to me about this. But maybe it's better this way.

My turn.

Madrid has been beautiful. The weather is great. Cool, sunny, and the *Biblioteca Nacional* conference has been good. I'm up for my talk in two days. I won't bore you with what I am going to say, and it won't be on the front pages of the newspapers, either.

The evenings are too long. Stuff is planned, like dinners, receptions, etc., but it seems like everybody knows each other from other meetings. I did meet an interesting "older student" (finishing her Ph.D. at the Sorbonne) last night at the Library exhibit. We just happened to be looking at the Dante manuscripts and soon found ourselves chatting about this and that. She, yes it was a she, speaks perfect English. Seems that all the Europeans know English but few Americans know European languages that well. We skipped the pre-planned dinner hosted by the Dante commission and went to the Sobrina de Botín for roast sucking pig and a carafe of Spanish wine. Then returned to the hotel. Period. Hey, you know, networking. Never know when I'll need some help in the *Bibliothèque Nationale*!

Aside from Hèlene, that's her name, I've had no other "romantic" encounters. So there!

On Saturday we went to the Escorial, Philip II's old mountain hideaway. About and hour's ride from the city. We went by bus on a winding road through the Guadarrama Mountains. There's a little town there, about 15,000 people, but the main attraction is the monastery originally built in 1557. That was the year that the Spaniards defeated the Muslims in the battle of Lepanto. Philip II built a monastery in honor of San Lorenzo and over the years he added to it. He wanted to be buried there. The library has some magnificent Arab manuscripts. The famous seat of Philip II, *la silla*, is up on a hill overlooking the monastery. That's where the king used to go to think and pray! You have to be an Olympic walker to climb the hill to see it. It was a day visit so we were back in the city that night.

Next day, ugh, we went to Toledo, famous for the El Greco paintings and the master's own house. This was a must. Put it on your list of great things to see and do. We went into some dark church, the lights went on, and in front of us was this magnificent painting called "The Burial of the Count of Orgaz." It took my breath away. The colors were so vibrant. It could have been painted yesterday.

I am rereading this and I sound like a tour guide.
Thinking of you, and I'll write again soon.
Promise, Promise, Promise.

ALAN

twenty-three

"So why did you write me only one letter?"

"*Only* one letter? That's one more than a lot of people got."

"Yeah, but you know what I mean."

"I do. But hey, gimme a break!"

"I literally ran to the mailbox each day to see if there was anything from you."

"So he wouldn't see it first?"

"That's a low blow."

"I apologize. I'm sorry."

"Are you?"

"Yes, I am."

"OK. OK. Forget it. Tell me. How does it feel to be back?"

"Weird."

"Weird?"

"Why do you keep repeating what I say? Don't you believe me?"

"Why are you so testy?"

"I'm not."

"Yes you are."

"OK. I am. I just feel funny."

"Funny to be back?"

"Yes. I think so."

"Maybe you were hoping everything would be different?"

"Different?"

"Yes, different. Like everything was changed. Not the same."

"No. I didn't think that. In fact, I was hoping that nothing had changed."

"It hasn't."

"So why do you feel funny? Everything's the same."

"Maybe when you go away for a while and live in another country, see other people, do other things, then when you return, your mind is still there and your body is here."

"Your mind is there only if somebody or something is keeping you there."

Alan didn't answer.

twenty-four

"You never told me about your reunion with Meg."

"You mean after I returned from Spain?"

"Yes."

"It was OK."

"Just OK?"

"They all met me at the airport. We went straight home."

"Were they happy to see you?"

"Sure."

"Did you tell her about Hélène?"

"Nope."

"I thought that transparency was the watchword of the modern marriage."

Alan smiled.

"I'm not quite sure that either party has to reveal everything." Alan drew out the word 'everything'.

Robyn added, "I guess we all have our little corners that we keep for ourselves and nobody else."

The only sound that Robyn and Allan heard for the next ten minutes was the cadenced crunch of their running shoes on the black gravel.

twenty-five

"I can never forget, how can I, your mad act of the heart when you stood alone under my balcony at midnight and played the love waltz that you had composed for me three years before. Your violin was bathed with tears and you played with such intensity that the dogs on the street and then the dogs all over the city began to howl. But then the spell of the music quieted them. You didn't see me but I peeked out of my window and caught sight of you walking down the dead street, not looking back...."

The theatergoers at downtown Boston's Ensemble Theatre laughed, then cried, and later grew silent, captivated by the dramatization of Gabriel García Márquez's novel, *Love in the Time of Cholera*. The Nobel Prize winner's story was staged by an avant-garde theater group that Alan supported financially but modestly.

When Alan saw the announcement of *Fermina and Florentino*, a theatrical presentation of García Marquez's latest book, he asked Meg to see it with him. Alan had never read anything by the Colombian writer, so this would be a painless opportunity to become acquainted with the current literary rage. And it meant a Saturday night out.

Every one of the theater's in-the-round seats was occupied when the 7:30 p.m. performance began. It was easy finding the assigned seats since only three rows surrounded the stage.

Neither Alan nor Meg noticed the couple that only moments before the performance started had slid into the row directly in front of them.

"You have been happy?"

    "Not completely. But who is? And you?"

    "My children are grown. My husband is dead. They gave my life meaning. Now I have to search for another me."

    "I had neither wife nor children. And although I loved the river and my career, I was never wedded to them. So I must still be searching."

    "Ah. We speak of things too serious. Old age, and death and families. Enough!"

Alan, Meg and the rest of the audience rode the roller-coaster of the first act. The hiatus of fifty years closed when the bizarre death of Fermina's husband, he fell out of a tree while chasing a parrot, allowed Florentino, the man who had kept loving Fermina for all those years, to show up at his wake. Alan was riveted on the drama.

"You symbolically cremated your husband, and that is as he wished. The spaces in your mind where you have managed to appease Dr. Juvenal Urbino are slowly being occupied by the field of poppies where you had buried your memories of Florentino Ariza."

The first intermission lasted for ten minutes. Alan and Meg stayed near their seats, standing and stretching. The couple in front of them headed for the bar at the theater's entrance.

    The second act was a flashback of sorts, rehearsing the bizarre lives of Fermina and Florentino, baring the loneliness that each had faced.

"She undressed me in the wink of an eye and in a single assault tried to satisfy the iron abstinence of her mourning. The gunfire kept whizzing over the roof and while we were in bed she kept going on about her dead husband's excellent qualities. She was convinced that he now belonged to her more than ever, in a coffin nailed shut with a dozen three-inch nails and two meters under the ground. And she said: I am happy because only now do I know for certain where he is when he is not at home. ...."

The woman in front of them laughed. There was no mistaking it. Alan and Meg were right behind Robyn and Eric.

Alan was upset. An awkward situation loomed. Meg, oblivious of Alan's predicament, was fixated on the drama unfolding on the stage.

After he got off the tram, I followed him down the street into Oil Lamp Alley. He stopped, turned around, and leaning on his umbrella with both hands, said:

You made a mistake, guapa, *I don't do that.*

Of course you do, I said, it's in your face.

I remembered a phrase that my godfather, our family doctor, once said regarding constipation. "The world is divided into those who can shit well and those who cannot." On this dogma, my godfather had elaborated an entire theory of character which he considered more accurate than astrology.–I put it another way. "The world is divided into those who fuck and those who do not." I distrusted those who did not: when they strayed from the straight and narrow path, it was something so unusual that they bragged about love as if they had just invented it. On the other hand, those who did it often lived for that alone. They felt so good that their lips were sealed because their lives depended on their discretion. They never spoke of their exploits. They confided in no one. They formed a secret society whose members recognized each other

*all over the world without need of a common language. That is
why I was not surprised at the girl's reply. She was one of us,
and therefore she knew that I knew that she knew.*

Alan's preoccupation with the inevitable encounter during the
next intermission prevented him from hearing Florentino
Ariza's soliloquy.

*"From Ángeles Alfaro I learned what I had experienced many
times without realizing it: that one can be in love with several
people at the same time, feel the same sorrow with each,
without betraying any of them. I remember saying to myself as
Ángeles Alfaro's ship was pulling out of the harbor: "My heart
has more rooms than a whorehouse."*

Alan only heard snippets of the affair that Florentino had with
his patient, Barbara Lynch.

*Once I had bitten, I could not let go of the bait. I visited her
daily. I could think of nothing else all day long but the time I
would spend with Barbara Lynch. I was too weak to stop. ...*

*After three months our love was ridiculous. Without time to
say anything, I would go to the bedroom as soon as I saw my
lover coming. To save time I wore no underwear, nothing,
believing that this would help him ward off his fear. No use!
Panting and drenched with perspiration, he would rush into the
bedroom, throwing everything on the floor, his walking stick,
medical bag, Panama hat, and he made panic-stricken love to
me with his trousers down around his knees, with his jacket
buttoned so that it would not get in his way, with his shoes on,
with everything on, more concerned with leaving as soon as
possible than with achieving pleasure. ... But he had finished on
time: the exact time needed to give an intravenous injection on
a routine visit.*

The Sunday that he didn't take communion was the day I became certain he was having an affair.

We went to bed. I heard her slow sobbing in the darkness, and she bit the pillow so that I could not hear her. I was puzzled because I knew that she did not cry easily for any affliction of body or soul. She cried only in rage. I dare not try to console her, knowing that it would have been like consoling a tiger run through by a spear, and I did not have the courage to tell her that the reason for her weeping had disappeared that afternoon, had been pulled out by the roots, forever, even from memory. She awoke and lit the bedside lamp. She spoke.

I have the right to know who she is.

I told her everything, feeling as if the weight of the world was lifted from my shoulders. I thought that she already knew, but she didn't. So as I spoke she began to cry again, not with her earlier timid sobs but with salty tears that ran down her cheeks burning her nightdress and inflaming her life.

Silence greeted the second intermission. Not the silence of boredom, but that of almost total enthrallment. The audience didn't want the scene to end.

Robyn turned and saw Alan directly behind.

"Alan," she said, "what are you doing here?"

The irrationality of the question surprised him.

"Same as you," he answered. He half turned to Meg. "Hey, have you met my wife, Meg?"

"I don't think so."

"Meg, this is Robyn Taylor."

Robyn held out her hand and Meg squeezed it lightly.

"Are you at Salem State too?" Meg asked.

"No."

Robyn wanted to add that she was the woman who jogged every day with her husband in the park. She was the woman who made Alan miss Kristin's rehearsal. She was the woman who almost went to Spain with Alan. She was the woman who was falling in love with her husband. But she didn't.

Instead, she said, "Powerful, isn't it?"

Meg took a second to realize that Robyn was talking about the play. She had half expected Robyn to introduce her to her companion. Or find out how Robyn knew Alan. Instead, Robyn changed the subject.

But Meg kept staring at Eric.

"Oh, I'm sorry," Robyn stammered, "this is Eric, my husband."

Eric smiled.

Alan shifted his feet.

"We're just going to the foyer to have a drink of something. Join us?"

"No, thanks," Eric replied almost too quickly, "we'll just stretch a bit here."

"See you later then," Alan said, and he and Meg moved towards the bar.

"Who was that?" Meg asked when they reached the foyer.

"Sometimes I see her in the park. Running. One of those people you pass every day and never get to talk to," Alan said.

Meg sensed that Alan was lying.

The flustered Alan never expected to meet Robyn and her husband. Robyn, on the other hand, wasn't as taken aback. She seemed to enjoy the irony of the situation.

The chimes sounded. Meg and Alan returned to their seats.

When they got there, Robyn and Eric's places were still vacant. Alan thought that Robyn might have steered Eric out of the building. Then they appeared, laughing, crossing the stage area hand in hand towards their seats.

As Robyn approached, she nodded, smiling at Meg and Alan. She and Eric sat down directly in front of them.

twenty-six

"Boy, you surprised me."

"I surprised *you*? What about you surprising *me*?"

"That was a coincidence of major proportions."

"Right behind us. God!"

"You know what? You seemed to enjoy it."

"I didn't. But it *was* sort of ironic."

"No, it wasn't. I almost had a heart attack. When I realized it was you in front of us."

"Oh, come off it. It wasn't that bad."

"How can you take it so lightly?"

"Take what? We 'run' together? That's all. Right?"

Alan didn't answer.

"Did you catch the part in the play when his wife confronts him about his affair with Barbara Lynch? When she says, 'And with a *black* woman!' As if that were the ultimate."

"How could I miss it?"

"They're so color conscious in Latin America. The Museo de las Americas in Madrid has these 18th-century drawings showing the offspring of different shades of brown and black. Color was and is a defining trait."

"And not here?"

"Of course, here too."

"Here the prejudice is more subtle, underneath the surface."

"So people in the north are more hypocritical about it. Than in the south."

"I think so. I think so."

Part Four
Cape Cod

twenty-seven

"People who have affairs rewrite the history of their marriage in order to justify their betrayal."

The pharmaceutical salesman sat back in his seat and waited for Alan's reaction. None came.

The salesman leaned towards Alan. "Do you buy that?" he asked.

"No. I don't," Alan replied.

"How come?"

"Because there may be an entirely justifiable reason for starting the affair."

"Again, please."

"A psychologist friend of mine once told me that there's a grain of truth in every stereotype."

"So?"

"So every affair has literally two sides to it. Maybe he wasn't meeting her psychological, or sexual, needs. Maybe he was too taken up with his career. She played second fiddle to everything. Or vice versa."

"Or maybe," continued Alan, "they were originally two very good people. And as they went on in life, she watched the kids grow up, she was there, but she always wanted to visit the places she heard of. She wanted to go places, do things. Maybe she wanted a career. Like him. So she developed a different vision of the future."

"And maybe he didn't see that she was unhappy."

"Or hear her."

"They got tired of fighting and really didn't make each other feel very good."

"So who's rewriting the history of their marriage?"

"Nope. That idea is too simple. It's more complicated than that."

Alan associated the idea with the tortuous emotions that overwhelmed him after he first kissed Robyn. They were running up the steep incline in the Back Bay Fens. When they reached the top, they were out of breath.

"Wait a minute," Robyn said, holding her sides. "I'm out of breath."

"Frailty, thy name is woman," Alan quoted Shakespeare.

"You're not exactly Mr. Health Club," she answered, bending over.

Then she straightened up, looking at him, still breathing hard. Her face was covered with perspiration and two wet spots on her back soaked through the T-shirt she was wearing. Alan noticed that the trees on either side of the path were still. The breeze ceased for a few moments and it seemed that the birds that lived there had left for lunch.

When Robyn straightened up, she momentarily lost her balance, lurching closer to Alan. She pulled her head back. Alan saw her wet, tanned face and lips. Robyn's long neck was unblemished. Her head was right next to Alan's. He put his arm around her waist, and said jokingly, "I'll save you." They were so close. Alan's lips moved towards Robyn's. She didn't resist. She closed her eyes and pressed her lips hard into his, then leaned her entire body into him. She felt him aroused. They stayed in each other's arms. Then Robyn turned quickly away, her head down.

"What's the matter?"

"No, no, no."

Tears began to well up in Robyn's eyes. Alan was surprised

that the woman he thought to be so strong was so vulnerable.

"When you touch me, I fall apart."

Alan thought that Robyn was exaggerating, but he didn't say that.

"Maybe we shouldn't see each other again."

Alan looked into Robyn's eyes and saw the answer.

"Nobody knows anything."

"Yet," she added.

"Kiss me again."

"Hey, Professor. Are you there?"

Alan heard the salesman talking to him at a distance.

"Those of you on the left-hand side can see clearly Martha's Vineyard down there. We'll be over Cape Cod on your right in a couple of minutes. And we'll be landing at Logan International Airport in about fifteen minutes, folks," the captain announced.

The crackling loudspeaker signed off.

twenty-eight

"You didn't answer me."

"Answer what?"

"My question. Do people rewrite the history of their marriage in order to justify their betrayal?"

"If you listen to a couple in the process of breaking up, you would think that they both have come from two different marriages. They see things so differently."

"Their filters were at work. They heard what they wanted to hear: Deborah Tannen, *That's Not What I Meant*."

"You're a walking library."

The salesman smiled and nodded.

"What if their home life was perfect? Or as perfect as it could be? Then what?"

The salesman in 6E slumped back into his seat. He shook his head. "Don't know. There has to be something that drives the guy to do something wild."

"Why?"

"Maybe just adventure?"

The salesman asked Alan if he personally knew anyone who had had an affair or was in the middle of one.

Alan didn't answer. Instead, he said, "Maybe they're afraid of dying."

"I never heard that one."

"You didn't? It's an old one. The guy keeps having relationships, always with younger women, to re-create his

138

youth. He doesn't want to believe he's getting older."

"That's a stretch."

"I'm not so sure."

Alan remembered the time that Robyn didn't show up in the park for her morning jog. Just a few weeks before. All sorts of crazy ideas ran through his head. Maybe house intruders were holding her hostage. Or she fell and was knocked out cold on the kitchen floor. Or maybe she had a fight with Eric after he found out about them. Alan threw caution to the wind and called her at home.

"Hello," Robyn answered with not a hint of crisis in her voice.

"Are you OK?"

"Of course I'm OK. Are you?"

"I was concerned. You didn't show up this morning in the park. I thought something happened."

"No, nothing happened. I'm still waiting for the roofer to come and replace a couple of shingles. So you'll have to hang up. He may be trying to get through."

"OK. Will you go to the park tomorrow?"

"Yes."

Alan detected a hint of annoyance in Robyn's voice. No matter. She couldn't have understood the concern he had felt, accompanying his sudden, overwhelming desire to talk with her, even if it meant that Eric answered the phone. Alan was oblivious of the consequences of his actions. He only thought of his next meeting with Robyn.

twenty-nine

"He hit your head?"

"Yes. He hit my head."

"With *his* head?"

"Yes."

"So I have to pay $250 for his emergency room costs?"

Kristin shrugged her shoulders.

"Is that all you can say, or do? Just shrug your shoulders?"

Tears welled up in Kristin's eyes. She didn't want to repeat the blow-by-blow account of how she had to slam on the brakes and how Justin lurched forward and hit his head on hers, causing a gash above his left eye. Then they drove to Mass General Emergency Room.

Alan grew more furious.

"That's what you get for fooling around in the car."

"I wasn't fooling around."

"Why wasn't Justin just sitting in the backseat? How come he was on his friend's lap?"

"There wasn't enough room for the five of us."

Meg intervened. "We'll send Justin's father the $250. So we'll keep it off our insurance."

"It's not the money," Alan insisted. "Kristin, you have to be responsible. You're driving tons of steel that can kill somebody."

"I know."

"It's not enough to know. Realize it."

Alan stomped upstairs, still irritated at Kristin and even more at himself for getting so annoyed. His temperament had become increasingly surly. That afternoon he shouted at the departmental secretary for turning "medieval" into "medeival" on his bi-monthly literature exam. And he did it in front of the two work-study students whom she supervised. Two days ago in class he had sarcastically suggested to a young co-ed that she read Eileen Power's *Medieval People* to learn about the 14-year-old who married a 50-year old merchant. It was as if Alan began to resent anyone with a youthful appearance. His look became belligerent and he began to daydream, thinking about nothing in particular, just drifting away.

"Where are you tonight?" Meg would ask.

"Nowhere," Alan lied.

thirty

"Don't be so snappy with her. She's only a kid."

"Only a kid?"

"God. Don't you remember when you were sixteen?"

"I do. And I was much more responsible too."

"Right. You're very selective in your memory."

"No I'm not."

"Sure you are. And besides, kids today have much more peer pressure to cope with."

"Please. Spare me. That's all the more reason to be a little careful when you have a car full of teenagers."

"Hey, put it out of your mind. At least for a while. We're still on for No Name's, aren't we?"

Alan hesitated a second. Then he answered, "Yes. Sure, we're still on. What time?"

"Good. Time? Let's see. How about a little earlier? Say around four."

"Four it is. See you there. You remember where it is, don't you?"

"How could I forget. I'll just get in line with the tourists if I get there before you."

"OK."

The step was a giant one. It wasn't lunch, or coffee, but dinner. In a public place with all the risks of being seen by friends, family, associates. Lunch or coffee could be sloughed off as spending a few minutes with a student or colleague.

Dinner was different. And his companion wasn't a colleague.

"Let's sit by the window facing the water," Robyn suggested.

"Sure."

The line outside hadn't been too long. Almost everyone was from out of town. Or at least it seemed that way. Why weren't the kids in school? Alan thought to himself. The kids viewed clambering over the construction apparatus of the Big Dig onto a Boston pier as an adventure. And a lot of them were there that day crawling over the piles of dirt like ants. The restaurant had started out as a little table where some Portuguese served the fish caught that morning. One table grew into two and before you knew it, a restaurant came to life. It had no name, so No Name's it became. A must on every tourist list, and equally shunned by locals. But it possessed the quality of anonymity that Alan and Robyn sought.

"I always liked this place."

"Me too, even though it's packed with tourists."

No Name's had undergone a recent metamorphosis. Gone were the red and white checker tablecloths, replaced by beige covered with paper that the waiters could zip off and throw away in ten seconds. Big blue fake fish were stuck on the walls. Like many U.S. restaurants, No Name's now catered to the fast-moving crowd, in and out, with a corresponding reduction of customer service. But it was still nice and the fish was always fresh.

By five o'clock it was getting dark. The city traffic grew with the late afternoon rush hour. Alan and Robyn watched the lights of downtown Boston go on one after the other. By five thirty they were sipping coffee.

"A little more," Alan offered.

"Half," answered Robyn.

Robyn put her hand over Alan's to stop him from pouring a full cup. But she kept it there and it stayed, hers over his, until he let go of the coffee decanter and slowly put his hand back on the table.

*

"It's almost 7:30. Where were you?"

"The time ran away with me. I didn't even look at my watch."

"Tom and Ellen were coming over to show us their slides of Turkey. You knew that!"

"Papers. Exams. I completely forgot."

"They're in the living room. I set up the slide projector two hours ago."

Kristin came into the kitchen. Her plaid skirt had a brown mud streak on the right side.

"What happened to you?"

"I fell."

"Fell?"

"We got off early from school and some of us went down to the pier, near No Name's, where they're building the tunnel."

Alan and Kristin looked at each other.

"We were fooling around and Missy Clark pushed me."

"Well, put your skirt into the clothes hamper," Meg said. "I'll take it to the dry cleaner's tomorrow."

Part Five
Logan Airport

thirty-one

"Common Mistakes that Throw Love into a Downward Spiral. I saw them on Netscape, you know, the Internet. They always mix in sex with the hot issues of the day!"

Alan was mildly interested in what the salesman was saying.

"What's the first?" he asked.

"Avoidance of problems. That leads to a downfall in the relationship."

"So says Mr. Netscape!"

"No. Not just Netscape. If you don't face a conflict head on, it's going to bite you in the end."

"Actually, I think that avoiding a problem is a wonderful coping mechanism."

The salesman didn't know whether Alan was serious or just being facetious.

"Surely, you jest."

"Nope, I mean it."

"Rome and the Catholic Church have successfully used this coping mechanism for centuries. Ignore the problem. It'll go away. Usually. I think," Alan continued, "that facing problems head on is a very American thing. Like a football game. Stand up to the opponent. Push him back."

"When something's bothering you, isn't it best to talk it out with your partner?" The salesman's voice had almost a pleading tone to it. "If there's a pattern in the avoidance, then you're not being genuine."

"It's not a question of genuineness. It's about peace."

The pharmaceutical salesman sank back in his seat.

The exchange was interrupted by the flight attendant's announcement.

"We're making our final descent into Logan International Airport. Please turn off all cell phones and computers. We should be landing in about twelve minutes. It's 10:33 a.m. The temperature on the ground is 58 degrees."

"It's unhealthy. The relationship would collapse."

"That's what we were taught in the '70s. Say what's on your mind. Confront. Clear the air. You'll feel better and the problem will be solved by discussing it. I'm not so sure that's the way to go."

"So keep it hidden? Festering. Then maybe by chance find out about it?"

"At the very least, it will keep the peace for a while."

"I doubt it. It will come to the forefront anyway. There's those little signs of an affair that always appear."

"Like?"

"Oh, I'm not going into them now. You know what I mean."

"No I don't. Tell me."

"Please buckle your seatbelts," the attendant said as she passed them. "We'll be landing shortly."

Alan was glad that the conversation was interrupted. His real thoughts were now elsewhere. In a few moments he would be seeing Meg and his family at Logan Airport. He would get off the plane, kiss them, and gather his luggage as if nothing unusual had occurred.

Flight 341 skimmed over the Atlantic Ocean, making its final approach to Logan. Alan and the salesman were looking out the cabin window trying to get a sense of place as they roared over the harbor. American Airlines Flight 341 landed without incident. As the jet rumbled down the runway and taxied over to the unloading ramp, before disgorging its passengers, both Alan and the salesman shifted in their seats tidying up before leaving the plane. They made the comments to each other that millions of other passengers had made before.

"Hey, maybe I'll see you in Copely Square."

"That'd be great. Have a good time in Beantown."

And that was it. When the plane came to a halt, the passengers stood, retrieved their overhead luggage, and waited for the doors to open.

Alan left the plane and outside the Security Gate he spotted Meg, Kristin, and Vicky.

They waved. He waved back.

thirty-two

On Saturday afternoon, at about 3:30, Alan had left the Gramercy Park Hotel without telling Robyn where he was going. He wanted to buy Meg a present, a keepsake from the Big Apple, and he thought that Robyn had best not know what he was up to. He would have preferred buying something at one of the trendy shops in Greenwich Village but time dictated that Alan head west towards Barney's on 18th Street. Maybe he would see something before he got there. He didn't. Minutes after entering Barney's, he spotted an off-white blouse, slightly on the conservative side, with long sleeves and pearl sequins embroidered on the front, a blouse that he thought was perfect. Alan bought it and was out of the store in ten minutes, heading back towards the hotel.

"Where did *you* go?"

"Out. For some air. How often can one walk around the Big Apple?" Alan said.

When he returned to Boston, Alan laid the blouse out for Meg.

"It's beautiful. I love it." Meg held it up to her chest and stretched out her arms.

"And it fits."

"You are so thoughtful. I think that this is the first time you ever came back from one of your trips with anything for me."

thirty-three

"So how was your flight back?"

"OK. Yours?"

"Good. A little bumpy around Providence, but OK."

"How did Eric's residency in New Orleans go?"

"Fine. Only one more left."

"And how was your weekend in New York?"

Robyn looked at Alan. She wanted to laugh. "How was my weekend in New York? Are you kidding?"

"That's what I said."

"You men! How do *you* think it was?"

"Fantastic! It was a fantastic weekend."

"I had sex with a stranger."

"A stranger? I'm not a stranger."

"There's so much about you that I don't know."

"That makes it all the more human, doesn't it?"

Robyn agreed, but she didn't know why.

"I feel like … I don't know."

"Say it. Like what?"

"Like I'm a device that you're using to get you out of your marriage with Meg."

"That's not true."

"Then why haven't you ever told me that you love me?"

"Robyn, you don't understand."

"I think I do. That's the problem."

151

thirty-four

"Why haven't you ever told me that you loved me?" The question kept echoing in Alan's mind. He even woke up to it in the middle of the night. But he never was able to reply.

Did Alan really love Robyn? Was he just fascinated by her beauty? Was he trying to recreate the romance that he once felt in Brookline? Was his affair with Robyn a symptom of a love that was already lost? After he saw the play, *Fermina and Florentino*, the dramatization of García Márquez's novel, he read the book and shook his head. Love lasting over 50 years? Was it possible? It sounded nice, but does it really happen?

Robyn's question meant that she was thinking hard about her relationship with Alan. He too thought. But his reflections took him in a different direction, almost as if he was preparing the scenario that would end their relationship. Or at least wishing that it would end.

thirty-five

A week after Alan and Robyn met in New York, the Boston Ensemble Theatre presented Connor McPherson's play, *The Weir*, at the same theater where Alan and Robyn had their accidental encounter. Half jokingly, Alan called Robyn to tell her he was going to ask Meg to see it with him on Saturday. The conversation was not what Alan expected.

"Alan, what's the big joke? Am I supposed to laugh? What exactly do you want from me?"

"Want from you? Nothing, absolutely nothing."

"Then what was New York all about?"

Silence.

"Aren't you happy with your wife?"

"Are you happy with Eric?"

Silence.

"Alan, where are we going with this?"

"Why do we have to be going somewhere? Can't we just enjoy each other?"

"Not that way."

"This is not a conversation for a telephone."

"Yes, it is."

"Can we get together and talk about it?"

"No, we can't. I don't know, Alan. I don't know. Maybe we should take a vacation from each other for a while."

Alan was stunned. "A vacation from each other?" he said slowly. "No, no, not at all. What do you mean?"

"Alan, I don't think it's working out. You and me."

"How can you say that? We just got back from New York."

"I just can't take all this indecision. All the ambiguity, and the deception."

"OK," he said slowly, "whatever you say."

Alan hung up.

When Alan went to the Back Bay Fens Park the next morning, he half hoped he would see Robyn. He didn't. However, one morning soon after, he did see her, walking with her two friends and Casco. He was sure it was her, even though he saw them from a distance. But he couldn't tell whether the two friends were the ones who were with her the first morning they met.

Reader's Guide

Alan Powell is a professor of Medieval Literature at Salem State College in Boston. He's married to Meg and has two teenage daughters. Robyn Taylor is married to Eric, a doctor studying for an advanced degree in psychiatry. She has one child. Alan and Robyn become running partners, they are avid joggers, and their friendship develops into an affair. Eventually, they spend a romantic weekend together in New York City.

On his return from New York City, (Alan and Robyn return on separate planes) Alan is seated next to a pharmaceutical salesman on his way to Boston for a meeting. The salesman's pointed questions trigger in Alan a series of reminiscences about the beginnings and unfolding of his affair with Robyn.

Why Alan chose Meg, or vice versa, what drives Alan's affair with Robyn, the deceptions, his relationships with his daughters, and the ambiguous denouement of his affair with Robyn hint at a tangled confusion beneath an apparently peaceful exterior.

Runners is a simple tale whose roots are deep in human history. However, scratch its surface and we find that its message is complex. Cushner presents us with a character from a Greek tragedy, a character who inflicts upon himself impending disasters he could have avoided.

*

1) RELATIONSHIPS. Is there anything in Meg's relationship with Alan that foreshadows an affair? Are the complexities and needs of one of the partners enough justification for an affair? Statistics now show that women have as many affairs, if not more, than men. Why could this be true? Can one be in love with (not just love) more than one person at a time?

2) EPIGRAPH. What can a 12th-century essayist like Andreas Capellanus tell a contemporary *homo sapiens* about love? Can love replace a love? What is implicit in the use of a Capellanus quote?

3) THE SALESMAN'S REMARKS. Agree or Disagree?

a) "...we choose this mate rather than that one because we think that we'll have stronger and healthier offspring." [Schopenhauer]

b) "Women see their *raison d'être* as motherhood, whether they're married or not."

c) "Do you believe in love at first sight?"

d) "Ever realize how many women say they were attracted to the guy because he made them laugh? You rarely hear that I was attracted because he was smart, or because he was kind."

e) "People who have affairs rewrite the history of their marriage in order to justify their betrayal."

4) TRAVELS. There are stretches of narrative describing Rome, Venice, and Madrid. What do the physical descriptions

of these places say about Alan's relationship to Meg? Does the physical setting enhance the social setting of the novel?

5) SALARIES. Meg's salary is higher than Alan's. Do you detect a deep-seated resentment on Alan's part about her higher salary? On the other hand, Alan says that confrontation and transparency only cause problems to worsen. Is there a consistency or a contradiction in what he says and what he actually does?

6) THE ENDING. What do you make of the end of the novel? Explain Alan's gift to Meg. Does the fact that Alan lays the receiver down slowly or allows Robyn to say that she can "take a vacation" from their relationship reflect Alan's true attitude? Is the affair over?

7) ROBYN. Robyn is a *mulatta*. Does Alan manifest a subtle strain of race prejudice in his relationship with Robyn?